E. B. Fleming, Augustin Fleming

Three Years in a Mad-House

The Story of my Life at the Asylum

E. B. Fleming, Augustin Fleming

Three Years in a Mad-House
The Story of my Life at the Asylum

ISBN/EAN: 9783337341121

Printed in Europe, USA, Canada, Australia, Japan

Cover: Foto ©Raphael Reischuk / pixelio.de

More available books at **www.hansebooks.com**

THREE YEARS IN A MAD-HOUSE

The Story of my Life at the Asylum, my Escape, and the
Strange Adventures Which Followed

E. B. FLEMING

AND

AUGUSTIN FLEMING

We talk of human life as a journey; but how variously is that journey performed! There are those who come forth girt and shod and
mantled, to walk on velvet lawns and smooth terraces, where every
gale is arrested and every beam is tempered. There are others who
walk on the Alpine paths of life, against driving misery, and through
stormy sorrows, over sharp afflictions; walk with bare feet and naked
breast, jaded, mangled, and chilled.—SYDNEY SMITH.

CHICAGO
DONOHUE, HENNEBERRY & COMPANY

DEDICATION:

PREFACE.

I here present you, courteous reader, with the record of a remarkable period of my life; according to my application of it, I trust that it will prove, not merely an interesting record, but, in a considerable degree, useful and instructive. In *that* hope it is that I have drawn it up; and *that* must be my apology for breaking through that delicate and honorable reserve, which, for the most part, restrains us from the public exposure of our own errors and infirmities. Nothing, indeed, is more revolting to English feelings than the spectacle of a human being obtruding on our notice his moral ulcers or scars, and tearing away that "decent drapery" which time or indulgence to human frailty may have drawn over them: accordingly, the greater part of *our* confessions (that is, spontaneous and extra-judicial confessions) proceed from demireps, adventurers, or swindlers; and for any such acts of gratuitous self-humiliation from those who can be supposed in sympathy with the decent and self-respecting part of society, we must look to French literature . . . All this I feel so forcibly, and so nervously am I alive to reproach of this tendency, that I have for many months hesitated about the propriety of allowing this . . . to come before the public . . . and it is not without an anxious review of the reasons for and against this step, that I have at last concluded on taking it.— From the "Confessions" of Thomas De Quincey.

TABLE OF CONTENTS.

CHAPTER I.

LIFE IN AN INSANE ASYYUM.

CHAPTER II.

I MAKE MY ESCAPE.

CHAPTER III.

GIVEN UP FOR DEAD.

CHAPTER IV.

THE BEGINNING OF MY WANDERINGS.

CHAPTER V.

A VARIETY OF ADVENTURES—LOST IN A TRACKLESS FOREST.

CHAPTER VI.

BLIND!

CHAPTER VII.

"YOU HAVE A DISEASE THAT WILL KILL YOU."

CHAPTER VIII.

I AM TOLD OF MY OWN DEATH.

CHAPTER IX.

OVERLAND TO MARLIN.

CHAPTER X.

STRUGGLES, INCIDENTS AND ADVENTURES.

CHAPTER XI.

"WHAT DID YOU SHOOT THIS MAN FOR?"

INTRODUCTION.

With the purpose of assisting the reader to a more perfect understanding of the truthful and authentic biography which is told in the following pages, it has been deemed expedient to give in this place a brief account of the events connected with, and leading up to, the narrator's imprisonment as a lunatic. This, for reasons which should be obvious to all, will be told in the third person. It is thought, or more properly, feared that the pronoun *I* has occurred much too frequently in the body of the work to make its introduction here anything but an error in taste.

The peculiar mania which affected the mind of Mr. Fleming, and which so altered the whole tenor of his existence, is probably ·best described by the term *melancholia.* The more immediate exciting causes were nervous depression arising from a disordered state of the system, and commercial reverses.

Mr. Fleming is a Georgian by birth and a Texan by adoption, having resided almost continuously in the latter state since *ante-bellum* days. Near the close of the old *regime*, as well as during the Reconstruction era, he was a dry goods merchant in the city of Jefferson, at that time the commercial center of northern and eastern Texas, with branch houses in Gilmer and in Sherman. In the year 1885 he had mercantile establishments in the towns of Sulphur Springs, Coffeyville, and Cleburne. But by reason of ill health, which necessitated the use of deputies or agents in all business transactions, and for other causes into which we need not enter here, financial reverses came upon him, and the various houses were closed by attachment.

One result of this unfortunate occurrence was the overturn of reason and of physical health. In a few months confinement and restraint became necessary; the order was issued; and in the spring of the year 1886 he was incarcerated in the North Texas Hospital for the Insane, at Terrell, Texas.

He remained as an inmate of this institution for about three years, and at the end of that time made his escape in some unknown manner, and for a number of years all trace of him was lost. In the following pages a brief account is given of his life at the asylum, with a number of interesting incidents which occurred there; the first truthful account of the manner of his escape which has yet been made public; together with the strange and unusual adventures which came after.

The authors of this volume entertain the hope that it may not prove wholly uninteresting, and that the time spent in its perusal will not be considered as having been utterly wasted. It is thought that the scenes and incidents which are so tamely described are of such a character as shall, in some degree at least, suitably recompense the reader and the purchaser.

It is to be understood, also, that the present volume is, in however small a degree, an answer to those many kind friends who have so urgently requested the preservation in book-form of some account of these incidents and adventures.

To the critic, if any such shall honor our little book with his notice, it is only necessary to say that any studied attempt at literary embellishment or effect is hereby distinctly disclaimed; and this may palliate —though it cannot wholly excuse—any serious faults or rhetorical or other inaccuracies or solecisms which may occur. We have not attempted to make literature, but simply a work which should possess general interest. We have written neither for the scholar nor the critic; but for the farmer, the laborer, the merchant, the lawyer, and for *all*, rather than for any individual or class of individuals.

Sulphur Springs,   AUGUSTIN FLEMING.
        March, 1893.

THREE YEARS IN A MAD-HOUSE

CHAPTER I.

LIFE IN AN INSANE ASYLUM.

His brain is wrecked . . . .
For ever in the pauses of his speech
His lip doth work with inward muttering,
And his fixed eye is riveted fearfully.
On something that no other sight can spy.

-MATURIN,

One morning in the spring of the year 1886, a carriage containing two men drove up to the huge gates which form the main entrance to the extensive grounds of the North Texas Hospital for the Insane, and signaled to the gatekeeper within. This personage responded with his usual promptness, and the two gentlemen alighted from their carriage and prepared to enter. While the gatekeeper is throwing back the ponderous gates, let us take a glance at the two arrivals. Their vehicle was covered with dirt and travel-stained, and had evidently been driven for many miles through a region of flying sand. The gentlemen themselves were tired and dusty, and stepped about with the manner of men whose limbs had been cramped and confined for a number of hours

15

within the narrow compass of a small vehicle. The elder of the twain was a tall, spare man, well on toward sixty, though his hair and beard were black as a raven's wing, while his dark and swarthy countenance had a more youthful expression than the face of his younger companion. The latter gentleman was scarcely fifty, but his hair was white, and his face, originally dark and sunburned, had now a sickly and ashen pallor. His eyes were restless and brilliant, and he had a trick of turning, twisting, and rubbing his hands together, sometimes with a bit of twine in his fingers, and sometimes empty, which he kept up without intermission. He spoke but little, and often, indeed, did not reply even when directly addressed. This did not spring from rudeness, nor from intentional discourtesy, but from the fact, which was evident to the most casual observer, that at times he was not conscious of anything going on about him. Now, however, after they had alighted from their carriage, and stepped about briskly for a moment to restore the circulation in their benumbed limbs, and had started toward the gate, he spoke:

"Dr. Taylor," he said, in a low nervous voice, darting a furtive look about them, "we have left the valise."

"So we have!" ejaculated the doctor; and he returned immediately to the vehicle and came back in a moment with a large valise in his hand.

As they passed in at the gate the keeper eyed them curiously, and said "Good morning," but he did not approach any nearer to them than his duties required.

They went on up a broad graveled pathway lined on
either side with tasteful shrubbery at a slow and leis·
urely walk—a pace which Dr. Taylor had never been
known to vary. The grounds through which they
passed were beautifully laid off and ornamented, and
had the appearance of being constantly swept and
tended. The graveled walk led up to the open doors
of a wide hall which pierced the asylum building in
the center, and ran through its entire breadth. The
building itself, a massive structure of red brick and
sandstone, loomed up, still ominous and frowning,
before them, and to one of them at least it had a more
gruesome a pearance than a sepulchre. As they advanced Dr. Taylor pointed out to his companion the
various objects which challenged his admiration, or
excited his curiosity, and freely expressed his pleasure,
wonder, or disapproval as the case might be. They
had now arrived at a point midway between the en-
.trance-gates and the hospital edifice, and some distance away toward their right the doctor remarked a
sort of inclosure or park surrounded by a stout plank
fence, and which afforded a cool and quiet retreat for
some two hundred men who were wandering to and
fro, or reposing beneath the wide-spreading boughs of
leafy shade trees. This scene attracted Dr. Taylor's
attention immediately, and he turned to his companion.

"Yonder," said he, "is the park where the patients,
under guard, of course, exercise themselves during
the day."

The younger man looked for a moment in the direction indicated, with a kind of fascinated terror, and turned his face away with a shudder.

No more was said until they reached the hospital building and entered the wide, cool, and lofty hall. The whole house was so still at the moment that one would have found it difficult to believe that he stood within the walls of an insane asylum. To their right as they advanced into the hall a little way was an oaken door on which was inscribed in gilt lettering, "SUPERINTENDENT'S OFFICE." Here they knocked, and a voice called out for them to enter. Dr. Taylor took his companion by the arm, opened the door and entered. They found themselves in a plainly furnished room, supplied with chairs, a desk, some books scattered about, a few portraits on the walls, and lastly in the presence of a rather stoutly built man with a short beard and a refined intellectual face. He rose at once and advanced to meet them.

"Dr. Wallace," said Dr. Taylor, "I have brought you a patient, Mr. E. B. Fleming, of Sulphur Springs."

"I am glad to see you, Mr. Fleming," said the distinguished superintendent, taking him kindly by the hand, and looking at him with keen penetrating eyes. "I hope your stay among us may be both pleasant and profitable to you."

The patient shuddered and cast down his eyes, but said nothing.

He was then given a seat while the two physicians withdrew to a corner and carried on a low-toned conversation for some time. At the end of half an hour

Dr. Taylor came forward and bade the silent patient farewell. They shook hands warmly and parted (though they knew it not) forever. Dr. Wallace then put a number of questions to the new-comer, and afterward turned him over to the attendants. By the latter he was shaved, put into a bath and dressed in the asylum uniform, a cheap suit of coarse grey with the words *North Texas Insane Asylum* indelibly branded upon every garment. This suit, which was chiefly remarkable for the fact that it did not fit the poor unfortunate who now donned it, and would scarcely have fit anyone, had the appearance of having been worn by every inmate of the asylum from its foundation down to that day. The trousers were some inches too short, but they were set off to great advantage by the pair of shoes now given to the patient in place of his own, and which were so large that he ran a pretty fair chance of sinking out of sight in their unexplored depth.

The ceremony of bathing (the typical lunatic has a holy horror of water, at all times and places, except when used for drinking purposes) and dressing over with, the transformed patient, not over pleased with his new suit,* was carried to the barber, and his tangled shock of hair cut close to his skull. His beard, which had been suffered to grow during the past quar-

* For some reason the law decrees that every applicant for admission into the Texas State Asylums shall be provided with three complete suits of clothes, three hats, and three pairs of shoes; and yet, if we are to judge by this instance, no sooner has the patient entered the hospital doors than he is stripped and compelled to wear a coarse and ill-fitting uniform supplied by the State. Perhaps, however, the real fault is to be laid at the door of greedy and avaricious attendants.

ter of a century, was long, wavy and luxuriant, but its venerable appearance could not stay the desecrating shears of the barber, and it was removed. But when the patient saw the barber's purpose he protested, and asked that his beard be allowed to remain. The barber, however, had his orders; and he bluntly replied that it could not be, and went on with his work. This cool treatment of his faltering but earnest request roused the poor lunatic's resentment, and he made a few vain struggles to break loose and rise from the chair. This resistance angered the barber very much.

"Do you want me," he roared, flourishing his razor aloft, "to cut your blasted throat? Are you a going to make me do it? If you are, it's all right. If you ain't ,why the h— don't you lie still?"

The patient, overawed by this terrific outburst, made no further objection, and the beard was removed.

.   .   .   .

Such, most courteous reader, was the manner of my entrance into the North Texas Hopital for the Insane, and such the place where I remained for three interminable years. Had the authorities told me in the beginning that they had doomed me to so long a stay, I should have been overwhelmed with despair; but I was encouraged by the hope that there would be no need for me to remain longer than a few months at most. At night I was locked into a narrow iron-barred cell, a light allowed me only long enough to disrobe,

my clothes, if such they could be called, taken from
me and deposited upon the floor outside my cell. All
lights about the building were put out at nine o'clock,
and it is not hard to imagine how intensely dark it
was at all seasons of the year, and even on moonlight
nights in our small stone cells with the doors closed
and the lights extinguished.

The asylum building, generally so still and silent
during the day, was a perfect Babel at night. As
soon as our candles were taken from us, and all the
lights about the building extinguished, the lunatics ·
in my ward, which was ward number one, would set
up a most tremendous howl. I dare assert that no
man can ever fully realize what dreadful and unearthly noises the human throat is capable of emitting until he has visited an insane asylum. Dozens of wild
voices would join in the weird concert which was
nightly carried on in the Terrel Mad-House—dozens
of maddened lunatics vie with one another in produc-
ing the most hideous sounds. No description can do
it justice—no imagination conceive the horror of it.
It is the nightly occurrence of this demon's concert
which transforms into frantic maniacs those unfortunates who, in the beginning, were quiet, docile, and
inoffensive.

They gave me medicines regularly; but it generally
cost the attendants a struggle to do so, for I dreaded
the medicine worse than any spoiled child, and would
not take it except upon compulsion. But rebellion
in a mad-house, as in a prison, is never tolerated,
and it is suppressed by such prompt and rigorous

measures that the delinquent does not care to repeat the offense very often.   Hence after several exciting conflicts with my keepers, in which I was badly worsted, and indeed severely punished, I took whatever they gave me without objection.

But my differences with those about the asylum were not entirely confined to the attendants. During the first few weeks of my stay, I had some trouble with quarrelsome lunatics.   Some of them would vex and annoy me by their pragmatic curiosity, or else would attempt to impose upon or bully me.   Indeed, regular fights were now and then occurring about the grounds, either between the lunatics themselves, or between them and their keepers.

One day I observed an imbecilic-looking lunatic, with the stature and frame of a giant, standing a short distance away who stared at me or peered at me in a most offensive manner, or he would come up to me with a great strut, touch me significantly upon the breast, and back away to his former position with many unnecessary and astounding contortions of the muscles of his body.   He repeated this ceremony, with some variations, and with all the pertinacity of a maniac until it became exceedingly annoying; hence I said to him:

"Look here, my friend, you be careful whom you put your hands upon!   You may go away and touch someone else, or touch the fence if you want to, but don't put your hands upon me again. They're dirty."

"And who are you?" said he, with the grin of an African gorilla.

"No one, in particular. I do not profess to be any-
body at all; but I am big enough to cuff your great
red ears for you," I said, somewhat fiercely, determined to scare him away if possible.

"Oh, you are!" he exclaimed, scornfully. "We
shall see if you are," and he advanced toward me as
he had done a dozen times already.

"You shall see!" I retorted, seizing a heavy stick
which was lying near; "you come any further, you
villain, and I'll brain you!"

He paused at once, looked at me with an expression of sickly terror for a moment, and then turned
and rushed away. It is needless to add that he did
not trouble me afterward.

This incident happened in the park, for it was here
that I was compelled to go with the other lunatics
every day, and spend my time taking exercise. The
park was small, but sufficiently large for the purpose
for which it was used. It was inclosed by a stout
plank wall some fourteen feet in height, and defended
upon the top by a guard of two strong steel barbed
wires. Here, in good weather, under the watchful
eye of a sufficient guard, the male lunatics spent
their time, and were allowed many liberties not
permitted elsewhere. Thus, though they might not
leave the park, unless they were ill, they might sit
down, lie down, walk,. play, or run, as the humor
seized them.

The insane negroes, too, walked in the park; but
they were allotted a certain part for their exclusive
use, and were not permitted to intrude upon that
portion occupied by the whites.

There were among us, as would naturally be expected, patients in every stage of lunacy, from the
most tragic to the most disgusting or ridiculously
comic. Even among lunatics, as well as everywhere
else, there are (if the expression be allowable)
"smart Alecs" and fools.

One gentleman, whose name I do not now remember, had become possessed with the idea that God
had "called him to preach;"—and preach he did, and
at all hours, it mattered not when, endeavoring to
edify his fellow lunatics with the most affecting sermons. And this whether they listened to him or not.
Most ministers, I believe, are governed in the
length and frequence of their discourses by the degree
of attention accorded to them by their hearers, but
it was not so in the present instance. Nothing could
damp his ardor—nothing induce him to remain silent.
On all occasions, possible or impossible, it made
not the least difference who was present, or what
was going on, this lunatic was giving out texts, beginning sermons or conducting prayer-meetings with
great fervor, and accompanying himself with loud
groans and sobs.

One afternoon he mounted a bench in the park,
gave out the text he designed to preach from, and
launched forth into a sermon that would probably
have lasted the whole afternoon. But the attendants, having orders to permit no patient to do or
say anything which might inflame their insane pas-
sions, at this point interfered and pulled the excited
lunatic down from his perch. This proceeding put

him into a violent rage; and forgetting, or not choosing to remember, his ministerial employment, he
swore a string of oaths most terrible to hear, saying:

"That the world had come to a h— of a pass indeed when ministers of the gospel could not preach
without being disturbed by pack of d— ruffians!"

This scene being ended, one of the meddlesome and
self-conceited lunatics that we have made mention
of, feeling no doubt that he must sustain his reputa-
tion for "smartness," ventured into that part of the
park allotted to the insane Africans. Having done
this, he gazed at the various negroes for a moment,
and finally walking up to the smallest and most in-
offensive-looking, began to abuse him roundly.
Whereupon the black lunatic drew back an arm which
discovered an astonishing strength in one so small,
and with one blow felled the meddlesome white to
the ground. This feat seemed to astonish the negro
quite as much as it surprised and discomfited his white
opponent, and the latter, with terror in his countenance, scrambled hastily to his feet and fled across
the park. Up to this point the negro had manifested signs of being ready to take to his heels himself, on finding what he had done; but now, with instincts essentially human, he turned and pursued his
fleeing foe.

The white men in the park, though lunatics to a
man, with the exception of the keepers, at this occurrence seemed to feel all the rancor of racial hatred
rising within them. So long as their fellow-lunatic

was so manifestly in the wrong they had shown no disposition to interfere with a chastisement so justly inflicted. But to see a white man fleeing before a negro foe, and the latter audaciously pursuing him into the midst of his friends, was too much for their self-control. The black, seeing among the whites certain signs which did not argue well for his personal safety, now turned and hurried back whence he came, with the slight difference that he got over the ground a little more speedily.

The angry lunatics, however, with loud shouts and execrations, rushed in a body towards the negroes. The attendants ran after them to preserve peace; but this was hardly necessary, as the blacks, after receiving but not bestowing a few blows, broke and fled in every direction, and frantically endeavored to hide, or crouched down beside the walls, some of them with hands uplifted and eyes rolling wildly toward heaven, moaned piteously; while all were well nigh overcome by the terror of the moment. The negro who had so rashly provoked the conflict was the worst frightened of them all. He rushed madly toward the nearest obstruction, with the intention of concealing himself behind it. He caught one or two blows as he ran, and these so greatly increased his fright that he ran with the speed of a deer; and finally, although no one had pursued him, he fell upon his knees and began to shout out a loud incoherent prayer. But ere this, finding their foes so little disposed to give blow for blow, or repel the assault, the maddened lunatics turned upon themselves, and a general fight ensued in which the attendants joined. The contestants bit, gouged, scratched, and gave and took many resounding blows ere peace was restored. None of the men were punished for participation in this fight, as during the struggle each man got enough blows to satisfy him for weeks to come.

*   *   *   *   *   *   *

Those who have had small or slight dealings with the insane can scarcely imagine the many artifices that some of them resort to to try the patience and forbearance of their friends. While it is vitally necessary to control the inmates of an asylum as with a rod of iron, it is necessary that the hand of steel be concealed under the softest of gloves. It is essential to the success of such an institution that the lunatic be given to understand, at once and for all, that the hospital rules must be obeyed, and that a violation of the least of them will result in speedy and inevitable punishment.

It may perhaps be well at this point to remark that no lunatic ever considers himself insane, and he resents most bitterly the idea of being considered such. Confinement in an asylum he regards as an infringement upon his personal liberty—an indignity designed to insult and humiliate him, and an act of base ingratitude upon the part of his friends. Like the drunkard in the play, he alone of all the world is sober, while all the rest of mankind are drunk.

This is a strange and oftentimes a ludicrous anomaly—an apparent paradox perh aps, in the eyes of many, yet the accumulated experien ce of age will sustain my assertion that it is true. The greater the degree of insanity, the more deeply rooted is the unhappy lunatic's conviction that though the world is filled with maniacs, his capacity for coherent thought and rational conduct remains unimpaired.

It is perhaps for this reason more than for all others added together that the lunatic is so hard to control. Their sincere conviction that their minds are sound, and wholly unaffected, contributes more than any other cause to confirm them in their perverse and obdurate opposition to the counsels of friends, relatives, or physician, and the contumelious rejection of all advice. Hence, by a course of reasoning peculiar to themselves, they are enabled to justify themselves in many deeds of cold-blooded violence, and to plan them with the studied duplicity of a professional assassin. The heart, therefore, of your lunatic friend, which appears so docile, tractable, and kind, may in its sceret depths be a perfect hell of fury and insane rage.

From this it may be inferred that the attendants in the insane hospitals are always in more or less danger of their lives, and at times they are compelled to be harsh, stern, and inflexible towards their charges. Often, indeed, it is only by the strong hand that they save themselves from the violence or malevolence of the lunatics, or quell their turbulent spirits.

Rows and disturbances were often occurring in the various dining-rooms as well as elsewhere. There was no general eating-apartment, or hall, for the use of the inmates collectively. Each ward had its own dining-room, though the meal-hour was the same in all. In my ward, where the more violent or obstreperous lunatics were confined, our dining-room was made use of by some forty or fifty of the inmates. It may be accepted as an axiomatic truth that man's animal instincts, in the degree according to which he possesses them, nowhere show themselves more plainly than at table. It is safe to assert that our good breeding, or the reverse, will tell its own tale in the dining-room. It goes without saying, therefore, that a party of lunatics at table presents a scene that cannot be said to possess many attractive features. On the contrary it is a disgusting spectacle, even at the best. The reader need not fear from this preface that we shall harrow his feelings by attempting a description of it. We shall content ourselves with simply requesting his attention to the following brief account of a conflict which took place betwixt the keepers and a lunatic a few days after my arrival. At dinner one day the lunatic referred to, who had never been known to be over scrupulous in regard to personal or general cleanliness, became incensed because a waiter had given him an unclean knife along with his fork and plate, and broke out into a loud and emphatic, though somewhat incoherent, objurgation of the delinquent. The knife which so excited his ire was spotlessly clean, and the attendant endeavored to convince him of this fact, but in vain. The keeper, realizing the folly of being betrayed into an argument with a maniac, cut the discussion short so far as he was concerned by walking away and going about his duties. The lunatic grumbled and complained for a while, but not very loudly until he perceived that no attention whatever was being paid to him. Whereupon, renewing his demand for another knife in a loud and vociferous manner, he worked himself into a great rage, throwing his arms and legs wildly about, his eyes almost starting from his head, while he ground and gnashed his teeth together in a manner at once vicious and bloodthirsty. He went on to declare, in the midst of inarticulate interjections and snarls, his fixed purpose of having another knife instantly or of perishing in the attempt. Some of the more timid lunatics shrank back from this ebullition of insane wrath; but the attendants, realizing the necessity of action, fell upon him in a body, and in the struggle which ensued bore him to the floor. Here they punished him without mercy, and did not leave off striking, kicking, and choking him until he was scarcely able to howl for mercy. They then forcibly replaced him at table, and during the remainder. of the meal he was the most quiet, docile and inoffensive man among us. I caught him now and then fixing his eyes upon the attendants as they hurried about the room intent upon their duties, with an expression compounded of hate, malice and superstitious fear; but whenever one of them approached him, he instantly sunk his eyes upon his plate and maintained a steady silence.

But while we were compelled to deport ourselves with proper decorum at table, more freedom was

allowed in the ball or dance-room of the hospital.
On Friday nights in the winter season every lunatic
who was physically able, both men and women, were
expected, or rather required (for no excuse would be
taken) to repair to the large hall where the dancing
was carried on   At such times the characteristic
perversity of the maniac showed itself to peculiar advantage, and came to the surface in many amusing
ways.   Most of the lunatics on these occasions obediently chose partners and endeavored to keep time
to the music.   But others, who could dance very
well, obstinately refused to do so, sometimes assign-
ing the most ridiculous causes for their refusal, and
again declining to vouchsafe any reason at all.   Far
more amusing, however, were those, both men and
women, who fancied themselves the most graceful
and elegant dancers imaginable, but who in reality
could not dance at all, nor could they be taught to
do so.   Their awkward and senseless movements on
the floor were supremely ridiculous, and excited a
great deal of laughter and ridicule.   But this they
would,mistake for applause, and it would so elate
them that they would cast aside all restraint, and
throw themselves about the room with all the frenzy
of wild Indians on a war dance, and yet with the so-
briety and gravity of a judge upon the bench.

*   *   *   *   *   *

Should the reader ask me what was the nature of
my feelings, or the state of my mind, in the earlier
days of my incarceration, I should answer: "Even
if I could tell, it would require too much time and

space to do so." However, I shall give a brief outline which may serve in the place of a more extended
description. Although at that time I believed myself
to be as sane as any man who ever walked the earth,
I could realize that *something* was wrong, either with
myself or with the world. I should labor in vain
were I to attempt to convey to the reader any adequate idea of the intense mental anguish I suffered.
The many and strange hallucinations which sprang
into being when my mind first lost its equipoise were
so real that nothing could persuade me that they were
merely the vagaries of my own brain. But the fan-
cies which occasioned me so much acute mental
torture and suffering—robbing my life of every joy,
and embittering my whole existence—was the thought,
or rather the belief, that some dreadful doom was im-
pending over me and over my family. Nor could I
rid myself of this impression. It pursued me night
and day, hung over me like the sword of Damocles,
and poisoned the few hours of peace that I might
have had. At all hours, both during the day and in
the long watches of the night, I could see my loved
ones in situations of the most terrible peril, calling
upon me for the aid I could not give.

The most dreadful scenes passed in solemn procession before my eyes,—mournful pageants—innumerable armies, passing and repassing, hour after hour,
with the heart stirring roll of drums, the rumbling
tread of marching feet, and wild sweet strains of supernal music. Many a time, when lying alone in the
darkness of my cell, I have seen the members of my

family borne by, loaded with chains or bound with
cruel thongs, with the shadow of some fate unheard-
of in its cruelty hovering over them. I accused myself
of horrible crimes—nay, I believed that I had murdered, killed and robbed—heard the stern sentence
of death pronounced against me, and in the darkness
and silence of night have listened with cold despair
for the expected footfalls of my executioner.

The reader may learn from this brief and imperfect
outline something of what I suffered. But this was
not all. Soon I came to believe that every inmate
of the asylum was my enemy, and that my companions were constantly laying plots to entrap and destroy me. Whenever, at any hour, I saw two or more
persons about the premises conversing together, an
incident that happened every day, I felt that they
were conspiring against me, and contriving pitfalls
into which I might stumble any moment. The gaunt
face of Death looked out upon me from every corner
and Destruction lurked in every by-way.

In fancy I saw myself convicted of revolting crimes,
and condemned to suffer the most agonizing and terrible forms of death which savage ingenuity could devise. I was dragged to the tops of mighty precipices
and hurled down to endless perdition, or seized, while
mocking and jeering laughter rang in my ears, and
cast into terrible lakes of fire, to be tossed like a
cork upon their waves, while dreadful tongues of
fire shot over me; and then, snatched by jeering de-
mons from the very jaws of death, I was hurried to
where huge cauldrons of boiling oil stood hissing and

seething over furnaces a hundred times hotter than fire, and held over them, while terrible voices shrieked in my ears that this was to be the manner of my death. Again I felt myself standing before open graves, in which something told me that I was soon to be buried alive, and suffocated under a mountain-weight of earth. Anon huge pits would suddenly open before me whose bottoms were lined with dagger-pointed spikes, and some irresistible weight seemed to press upon me and bear me down upon them.

Often during the stiller hours of night dreadful voices would call out to me and accuse me of committing atrocious crimes, and in time I came to believe this, and that my wickedness really deserved some punishment. Then I concluded that the asylum was full of keen and merciless detectives, sent there to secure proofs of my guilt in order that death in some barbarous form might be meted out to me; and I soon came to realize that I was subjected to a constant and sleepless espionage, which could only result in the detection of my guilt.

The reader will readily imagine —if he is not already too wearied with these small details to imagine at all—that under these circumstances my life was a torture and my existence a dreadful burden. Hence I resolved to destroy myself. This resolution was no sooner formed than I took steps to put it into execution. It was easier, however, as I soon ascertained, to plan a suicide in the asylum than to carry it out, as it seemed that the Superintendent, Dr. Wallace, had suspected me of such designs from the first.

By his orders I was watched, and several attempts at self-destruction proved abortive. I was determined, however, and with all a madman's cunning, I waited my chances. Not a great while after this, therefore, I contrived to purloin a large cake of laundry soap and secrete it upon my person. At the first opportunity I broke the soap into smaller pieces and swallowed them. It was a nauseous dose, as I need hardly say, but I should·have swallowed a porcupine had it been possible, if it would have freed me from my misery. The soap did not kill me, but it made me so deathly sick for a few hours that I thought my end was near. Yet it was not so, for it only added to my misery without abating any part of it. The suffering it caused me was pretty considerable for a few days, but it finally passed off, leaving me no worse for my experience. I learned at the time, and have never since forgotten, that laundry-soap, as a means of lessening the ills of life by stopping its machinery, is a dismal failure.

This attempt, like the others, having proved to be so hopeless a failure, it might be supposed that I should have given the idea over, with no better means at hand for affecting my purpose. And so, probably, I should ; not out of choice, but from ne-cessity, had I not been fortunate enough a week or so later to find a part of an old beer-bottle buried in the sand. This circumstance opened a way for the accomplishment of my design, and I concealed the bottle as I had done the soap, in the pockets of my jacket. I afterwards broke the bottle into small pieces and swallowed them. When this was done I had no doubt that it would be impossible for me to survive for more than a few hours, and I waited with no little anxiety for the appearance of those symptoms which should announce the approach of dissolution. But to this day, seven years later, no such symptoms have made their appearance, and I waited in vain. Indeed, the swallowing of the pounded glass gave me no inconvenience whatever. ·When finally I began to realize that the pounded flint had caused me no injury, I could scarcely believe the evidence of my own senses. I had always supposed, without thinking much about the matter, that beaten glass swallowed in this manner was as certain to cause death as a cannon ball, properly aimed. I know now that there are many persons who would not be incommoded in the least by the presence of broken glass in the stomach, while others could not survive such a catastrophe more than a few hours. In my own case, however, the truth compels me to state that the soap came nearer killing me than the glass.

This last failure decided me, and as long as I remained an inmate of the hospital, I never renewed the attempt. Whether I did so afterwards remains to be seen.

But, while I no longer meditated self-destruction, my mental sufferings were as acute as before; and I studiously avoided the Superintendent, and all those whom I believed to be spies. Often, however, in walking about the asylum building, or through its corridors, I came suddenly upon Dr. Wallace, who went

to and fro upon his official duties. To my suspicious temper it appeared that he always looked upon
me curiously, and with a glance which penetrated
to the innermost recesses of my soul, and read like
an open book every hidden thought and impulse.
These casual meetings always greatly alarmed me, for
I thought I saw in them conclusive evidence of their
design to penetrate into all the secrets of my life.

In reverting for a moment to my mental record of
those gloomy and despairing years, I find myself wondering at the considerate care and kindness, as well
as the calm and benignant temper that invariably
characterized Dr. Wallace's demeanor, as well as that
of his great-hearted associate, Dr. F. S. White, towards the unhapppy but patience-trying lunatics.

At this point I am reminded of the fact that visit-
ors, most generally, I believe, of the female sex, were
coming to the hospital at nearly all hours. Some
of these had relatives or friends whom they wished to
see, while others came out of mere curiosity. Many
sad and pitiful scenes occurred in the parlors during
the visits of these ladies, many of whom had hus-
bands held in restraint. To some of the male lunatics these brief calls were sources of pleasure greatly wished for and long remembered. Often I have
seen their worn faces light up with feverish but timid
hopefulness when a female form was seen entering
the parlors, and I have watched them sink back into
a dull apathy of despair when the minutes passed
and no summons came for them. There were others
who dreaded these visits greatly and looked forward

to them with nervous apprehension. Indeed, any such, when they had warning that a summons would presently come for them from the parlors, would endeavor to conceal themselves, and had to be brought in by main force.

A keeper came to me one day to announce the fact that two ladies were awaiting my presence in the parlor. Wrapped up as I was at the moment in my own melancholy thoughts, I was ungracious enough to say that I did not wish to see them. No choice in the matter, however, was given me, and I followed the attendant obediently enough. The ladies rose on my entrance and asked me if I knew them. I replied that I did, but that I was not receiving lady callers that day. At this rude and ungallant speech the ladies laughed heartily, in which they were joined by Dr. Wallace, who was present. Strange to say, I was the only one in the room who became offended. But their laughter *did* offend me, very much, for not being at the moment conscious of having done anything wrong, I thought they were making sport of me!

Of course the lunatic men and women were carefully kept apart, and were never allowed together except when they met by accident or in the hospital dance-room. When they came together here, many comic as well as ridiculous scenes occurred, besides those which have been mentioned. For it must be remembered that in nearly all cases the male lunatic loses all that natural gallantry and reverence for the fairer and gentler sex that is so characteristic of every true man who is in his sober senses. If any woman present did anything to bore or disgust a lunatic, he did not hesitate to tell her so, without stopping to bother himself about a choice of words.

Thus I have often heard conversations something like the following. One night a quiet-looking lunatic, disgusted at the unmaidenly conduct of one of the women present, said to her:

"You are a fool. You haven't got any sense, and you make me sick. You go away from here," and with that he put forth his hand and pushed her back.

Nothing abashed, however, the woman clung to him, saying fondly, though very likely they had never met before:

"But I love you, dearest. When are you going to marry me?"

Giving a snort of disgust, and endeavoring to break away from her, the lunatic replied:

"I will never marry you. I don't want you. I wouldn't *have* you. You aint got no sense."

At this the fair Helena protested, and a sort of scuffle ensued, she expostulating with fond persistence, and he endeavoring to unclasp her detaining hand and escape. Finally, however, she became enraged, and forgetting the ardent love she had professed but a moment before, she abused him in strong terms and, even gave him a blow or two by way of emphasis. The attendants finally were compelled to interfere, and bear the shrieking and struggling Helena from the presence of her disgusted Demetrius.

On another occasion, when the lunatics were re-

turning in a body to dinner, at the noon hour one
day, a woman broke from the body of females who
were filing towards the house on the opposite side
of the grounds, and eluding the outstretched hands
of her keepers, she ran madly towards the column
of men a hundred or so yards away. The peculiarity
of her disease was, as I afterwards learned, that she
was constantly in search of a mythical husband, and
whenever she discovered him, as she did nearly every
day, a terrible scene of hysterical joy and obstreperous delight would ensue.

The woman ran towards us shrieking as she came,
her long hair flying in the breeze, and her eyes gleaming with insane fire. She removed her clothes as
she came, throwing each garment wildly aside, and
rending at another in order to remove it with the least
delay. By the time she reached us she was entirely
nude, the white flesh of her naked body showing with
startling distinctness against the dark back-ground
of earth and trees, while her clothes were scattered
at unequal distances along the ground for a space of
two hundred yards. With a wild scream of joy she
rushed forward and sprang upon the largest lunatic
among us, clinging to him frantically, with a grasp
that would not be shaken off, crying:

"O my husband—my husband—my dear, precious
husband! I have found you at last!"

"Go away, woman!" ejaculated the lunatic, struggling to free himself; "I do not know you. Go
away!"

"O my husband!" she shrieked, and clung all the
tighter.

They struggled back and forth for a time, and the big lunatic contrived to free himself, and step hastily back. But she rushed upon him again and managed to seize him in a tighter grip than before. He struggled manfully, but could not free himself. He cursed her in vigorous English, while her frenzied shrieks rose high and shrill. Some one finally caught her, and the man released himself and fled towards the house. She pursued him wildly and, in frantic despair, filling the air with her shrill screams.

Seeing that she was about to overtake him, the big lunatic stopped, faced about, and picked up a brickbat that was lying near. He drew back his arm with a look of determined fury.

"I'll kill you," he yelled, "you she-devil! If you come another step, I'll crush your head with this brick!"

But she came on in spite of his threat, and the enraged man would have struck her with the brick had not an attendant at that point interfered and restored peace by seizing the woman, holding her until help could arrive, and then bearing her bodily from the grounds.

* * * * *

One of the strangest features in a lunatic's character is curiosity. This faculty seems to grow at the expense of the other faculties, and it sometimes attains to enormous proportions. It is manifested in many curious and ludicrous ways. Those who possess an unusual share of it—and they are generally the more harmless ones—pass their time in prowling and poking about the asylum premises. They examine such things as seem to strike their fancy with the simplicity of a child, and they are often observed gazing curiously, wonderingly, but sedately at their fellow-lunatics, just as though they presented the most attractive sight in the world. Often they try the patience of the more gloomy and violent maniacs very greatly.

I have seen one of these latter in some corner of the park completely surrounded by a crowd of the harmless ones. They would stand or sit about him in a perfect swarm, looking at him curiously, and watching his every movement with the most owl-like gravity. Some would stand while many would seat themselves upon the ground, but no word would be spoken and not a sound uttered. In perfect silence they would sit or stand, gazing at their gloomy fellow-lunatic as though they thought him the greatest curiosity in the world. In return, the object of this strang espionage generally feigned to be unconscious of their presence, and for whole hours neither side would utter a word. The harmless lunatics, however, unable to restrain their meddlesome and prying proclivites, would draw closer, some of them perhaps plucking at their victim's sleeve, or otherwise disturbing him. Whereupon, he would turn upon them with savage fury, and, scrambling frantically to their feet, they would run for their lives, the perfect picture of ludicrous terror.

On one occasion—and many of this kind happened to me—I was seated in a retired corner of the park

conversing with a friend (who had lately been confined as a lunatic) named Smith, or at least we will
call him so. We had not finished our conversation
when a number of the harmless lunatics that we have
referred to, their curiosity getting the better of them,
came and squatted down in a circle around us. They
watched us curiously, but very gravely, and in perfect
silence, as was their custom, dividing their time between gazing at us and industriously drawing all sorts
of fanciful figures in the sand, or digging miniature
wells, with pieces of broken sticks. This surveillance
became very annoying, and we turned our backs
upon them.

This manœuvre on our part puzzled them for a
while, as they wished to bestow their whole attention upon our faces and not our backs. Evidently
they were greatly perplexed as to how to meet such
a contingency, and did nothing at all for some moments but puzzle their beclouded wits in an endeavor
to find some way to check-mate our unexpected
movement. Finally two of them rose and came up
to within a yard of us, without uttering a word, and
bent their heads towards us in listening attitudes.

My friend Smith became great annoyed.

"You go 'way," he said, pushing them back, not
very gently. "We don't want you here; you are
fools."

This, as may be supposed, had no effect on them
whatever, especially when uttered by a lunatic who
was much nearer imbecility than they had ever
been; hence we left them and retired to another

corner of the park. They followed us at once, and formed another circle, squatting upon the ground, and maintaining a steady silence. The same incident was repeated, with the slight exception that Smith became enraged and knocked one of them down, whereupon they fled as fast as their terrified legs could take them, and thereafter only watched us from a distance.   ●

*   *   *   *   *

Of the many lunatics confined in the North Texas Insane Asylum, probably a large proportion of them had lost their minds through intense meditation on religious questions. One of them whom I particularly observed had for some time been declaring his belief in his ability to fly, with no other wings than his arms. Yet so far he had never actually attempted to do so, contenting himself with boasting, and with the long flights that he every day took in fancy. He did not, however, give up the idea, as will presently appear.

Believing that he had only to make the attempt in order to find himself able to fly to heaven, he climbed one day when no one was looking upon the roof of a small building in the park. Perching himself upon the edge of the roof, he stretched out his arms, gave a great "flop" with them, and sailed out into space. But he found that flying without wings was a hazardous experiment, as it chanced that "space" into which he sailed with such confidence was merely the space between the roof of the house and the ground. He fell headlong to the earth, where he lay as one dead, without motion or sign of life. He had no sooner struck the ground than the attendants, with exclamations of horror and dismay, ran to him and raised his limp form from the ground. The fall however, had not killed him, strange to say, but had done no greater damage—which was sufficient— than to break his leg, and (what was most wonderful of all) the shock restored his mind. He recovered in due time and was discharged. I never saw him afterwards, but I felt sure that he had learned a useful lesson.

There was in the asylum at this time a young woman whose history was one of the saddest I have ever heard. My attention was attracted to her by her peculiar behavior, and by inquiry I learned the melancholy story of her life. It was short, for her years were few; but it was pregnant with unhappy incidents. I had noticed her at times decked out in what she fondly thought was bridal array, and learned that she spent a large portion of her time before her mirror, ornamenting her person with all manner of wedding finery. Each morning, in fond anticipation of the marriage ceremony which was to be performed that day, with herself as bride, she would make an elaborate toilette, and manifested the greatest anxiety in regard to the fit and appearance of her apparel. Then, when the bridegroom did not come at the expected hour, she would wander about the place with a far away look in her eyes, yet with such a hopeful and pathetically expectant air until the close of day, that no one had

the heart to undeceive her. When night came, she
would quietly begin her preparations for the morrow's
bridal; and though days and weeks and even years
had gone by, and still the groom came not, she never
lost hope, nor despaired, nor ceased her constant
watch for him. But alas! he for whose coming she
thus waited, day after day, had long since journeyed
whence none ever return; and while she thus passed
her time in waiting for his hand-clasp, and listening
for his footfall, his body was mouldering to dust in
a far-off grave. When she saw each day that he
did not come, she did not grow weary nor complain,
but only smiled, with a sadness more pitiful than
tears, and said that she knew he would come; and
so the days passed on. Her extraordinary hopefulness under continual disappointment, and her brave
though saddened resignation, were not the least
among the features of her strange character and,
seemed to spring from a fountain which nothing could
exhaust.

Her story is here given, though briefly, both for
its interesting features, and the palpable lesson it
conveys. As her exact name is really of little consequence, and many of her relatives are still living,
let us call her Ellen Smith.

At the time I saw her she was near twenty years
of age, though the incidents I am about to relate
occurred some two or more years before. Her father
was a prominent and well-to do farmer, and Ellen,
his only daughter, was the pride of his life. She
was a beautiful and intelligent girl, very popular

among all classes in her native county, and as thoroughly accomplished as the lavishly expended means of a fond father could make her. As she grew up her beauty increased, and many good qualities of mind and heart along with it. It need hardly be said that she had a great number of devoted admirers, and it was astonishing to see what abject slaves she made of them. There were many indeed who manifested such a romantic and chivalrous attachment to her and, showed so much perturbation and distress whenever she exhibited the least sign of displeasure, that they were both pitied and laughed at.

In time, however, she became betrothed to a young farmer in the community namd James Robertson. He was a quiet, modest, and unassuming young man who loved her very fondly. Although young he had been thrifty and industrious, and had acquired a comfortable home, and much valuable property lying near the homestead of the Smiths. The other suitors, finding themselves outdone by their modest young rival, and seeing that every hope was lost, retired in despair, leaving a clear field for the victorious young farmer.

Regularly every Sabbath morning James Robertson rode over to the home of his *fiancee* and passed the day with her, only returning through the quiet country woods to his bachelor quarters when the old-fashioned clock upon the mantelpiece warned the young couple of the approach of Monday. The young farmer's intense and consuming passion for Ellen was well known in the neighborhood, and it was believed that the loss of her love would overturn his reason, or cause him to commit some desperate deed. Of this Ellen was perfectly well aware, and it is probable that she did not have that love for him that she supposed, or that he expected and demanded. The fiery vehemence of his own love was so intense and exacting as to be painful alike to both, and doubtless so operated, more than any answering fire in her own breast, as an influence in his favor. The chances are that when she had daily such evidences of the consuming intensity of his passion, that its very force pleaded more strongly with her than any love in her own breast.

However this may be, everything seemed to promise a future of Utopian happiness for the young couple, and many a maiden in the quiet country neighborhood looked upon the progress of this apparently perfect love with mingled feelings of awe and envy. Young Robertson was so happy, and his life so full of joy, that he could not conceal his ecstasy, and his plain but honest face had softened and taken on a new beauty that was wonderful to see.

But in the course of a few months, a new character appeared upon the scene that was destined to work irreparable woe. This character came in the person of a young man named Albert Harrison, who came into the secluded neighborhood early in the autumn. He was a handsome, dashing and agreeable young man, and he soon made devoted friends of half the community. A gayer or more rollicking young gentleman had never been among them, or one more able to creep into the affections of young and old with such surprising quickness. He adored the gentler sex with outspoken fervor, and had so soft a spot in his own gay heart for them, that he had no difficulty in finding his way to theirs.

In an evil hour he became acquainted with Ellen Smith, and from the first day of their meeting it became evident to all that they had formed a sincere and mutual attachment. Young Harrison after that became a frequent and open visitor to the homestead of the Smiths, and in a comparatively brief space of time his engagmeent to Ellen was publicly announced. When this intelligence reached James Robertson (and you may be sure that it was conveyed to him with very little delay), he indignantly denied its truth, and repelled the insinuation upon his lady's good faith with such vehemence that his acquaintances soon became chary of mentioning it to him at all. Nevertheless, in spite of his brave denial of the story, it gave him no little uneasiness; and at the first opportunity he mounted his horse, and rode immediately to the home of his affianced wife.

At first she refused to see him, and at this his heart sank within him; but his perseverance overcame her scruples, and she met him in the parlor. Here he gently and cautiously told her the nature of the story that was going the rounds of the neighborhood, and questioned her upon it. Such was her infatuation for Albert Harrison, that she boldly and flatly told James Robertson that she had plighted her troth to him. Astounded and indignant, he endeavored to reason with her, but so completely had the luckless girl forgotten her duty and her honor, that nothing he could say succeeded in rousing within her a single feeling of pity for him, or repentance for her conduct.   A stormy and passionate interview ensued, and at its conclusion Robertson strode from the house mad with despair, and returned to his home.

Meantime, preparations for the wedding went on and Ellen, in spite of the entreaties, remonstrances, or even commands of her relatives and friends, steadily refused to reconsider her determination to become the wife of Albert Harrison.   As for James Robertson, he went about his business very much as usual, and was never heard to utter a word of reproach against his faithless bride, or a threat against his successful rival. It was remarked, however, that he was quietly disposing of all his property, and .converting everything he possessed into ready money.

The wedding ceremony was to be performed at eleven o'clock A. M. one Sunday in October.   On the morning of that day, Ellen stood before her glass decorating her person with that beautiful and fascinating finery which is at once the pride and despair of every female heart.   Her mother, and several of her young girl friends were flying about in a great state of excitement, or bending over the bride to pin this and arrange that, while Ellen, in a perfect flutter of delicious excitement, yet with a strange sinking at her heart (she had such sensations often now), ordered her assistants about like the imperious little autocrat she was, or admired her pretty face in the mirror.

When all was done, and the great work of dressing for the bridal was actually accomplished, the girl walked with immense dignity (in her character of *bride*, which gave her a greater importance in the eyes of all women than if she had been elevated to the Presidency itself), to and fro across the room, to listen to the semi-critical and wholly admiring comments of her friends, and with the ostensilbe purpose of ascertaining "how she looked," though she knew perfectly well that she looked irresistibly bewitching.

They were expecting the appearance of the bridegroom every moment, and Ellen had sent the girls out two or three times to stretch their fair necks in an endeavor to catch a sight of the expected groom, when the rapid beat of a horse's hoots rang out on the crisp autumn air. On hearing this, the girls hastened immediately to the door. A horse, covered with dust and foam, dashed up to the gate, his rider pale and trembling, and bearing visible marks of perturbation and excitement.

But for the present we must leave this scene, in order to relate the adventures of the bridegroom. He had a number of miles to ride before reaching the home of the Smiths, and had accordingly mounted his horse and set forth quite early, accompanied by some half dozen young men. The road they pursued led through a forest all the way. They rode along gayly, passing the time in laughter, song, and animated conversation. In passing a spot where the road made a sharp turn, and a great mass of tangled undergrowth lined one side of the highway, a human figure put aside a mass of overhanging vines and stepped out before them. The bridegroom rode in front, and the intruder, who bore a long gun in his hand, called out to the cavalcade to halt. They did so mechanically, most of them meanwhile recognizing James Robertson in the man before them, but so wild, unkempt and haggard that hardly a feature resembled those of the man whose happiness, so short a time before, had been the talk of the neighborhood.

"Gentlemen," he said, in a voice they had never heard before, his dry lips working convulsively, while his eyes glared with an expression that was terrible to see, "I would ask of you that you all remain here in this spot as witnesses to what I shall say to this man," waving his hand towards the bridegroom, whose face had grown white with fear.

"Albert Harrison," he continued, with a dreadful calmness, and without giving anyone time to reply, while the young men looked at him, and at the groom, and at one another, in amazed and wondering silence, "you have triumphed over me, and trampled my happiness in the dust. You have stolen my love from me, and ruined my life forever, for without her I do not care to live. You have done all this, and without feeling one sentiment of pity for me. Even now you are on your way to go through with the ceremony that shall make my wife your bride. But your treachery will avail you nothing, for your hours are numbered! If Ellen Smith cannot be mine, by the God who rules above us, she shall never be yours!"

The countenance of Harrison, during this address, had turned to the hue of death, and with trembling hands and faltering tongue, he begged the enraged man in piteous tones to spare his life.

The only answer that Robertson returned was to glare on his rival with a look of mortal hate, and aiming his gun at him, he shot him through the heart. He then turned back into the silent depths of the forest, and was never apprehended, or even heard from afterwards.

Harrison had fallen from his horse, and now lay, a bloody and lifeless figure, in the dusty road. His horrified friends sprang from their horses and raised the unfortunate man's head, but life was extinct. One of the young men was sent in hot haste for a physician, while another bore the sad news to Ellen Smith. She was standing, as we have seen, in the doorway, as the messenger galloped up. As soon as the miserable girl could be made to realize that Albert was dead, and by whose hand, she fell to the floor in a swoon.

She was roused with great difficulty and only after long hours of anxiety and suspense. But with the return of consciousness it was found that her reason had fled. She became a hopeless and incurable maniac, and in the course of time was incarcerated in the Terrell Asylum.

This is the brief story of the melancholy life of Ellen Smith.

It is fitting, in bringing this chapter to a close, that we speak of the death and manner of burial of those who die at the asylum. Of the large number of unfortunates who are yearly confined there, there are many who never leave it alive. Those that die, as a general rule, are buried on the premises by their fellow-lunatics. Death is always a melancholy thing; but to die far away from home, among strangers, and at a time when the mind has become clouded, is a dreadful thing indeed. To me, it was always a sad and solemn occasion when any of my associates died. Yet no regular funeral, in the common meaning of the word, is given to these unfortunates, such as we of the outside world always have on such occasions. Indeed, this is impossible, and the corpses of such as are to be buried at the asylum are interred with very scant ceremony. The manner of such burials might remind one of the interment of Sir John More, in Wolfe's immortal lyric:

> "We buried him darkly at dead of night,
>   The sod with our bayonets turning;
> By the struggling moonbeam's misty light,
>   And the lantern dimly burning."

The corpse is hastily inclosed in a cheap pine coffin, and in the night, without friends or mourners, the grave is dug, the coffin lowered, and the damp sod thrown in upon it. In this lowly and humble manner, within the precincts of the hospital grounds, many an unfortunate is mouldering to dust; and thus has no doubt ended the mortal career of many who somewhere in the unknown past began their lives with high hopes and burning ambition.

CHAPTER II.

Oh! give me liberty!
For even were paradise my prison,
Still I should long to leap the crystal walls.
                                    . *Dryden.*

As the title of this volume indicates, I remained an inmate of the North Texas Hospital for the Insane for three years, or nearly so; and as the discerning reader has no doubt perceived, I did not believe that my mind was affected. Hence I felt that my imprisonment in the asylum was a great injustice to me— indeed, an almost inexcusable wrong against my rights as a law-abiding citizen. I was well aware that my family and friends considered me insane, and the Superintendent of the asylum also. But I *knew* that my mind was sound, and I had tried in vain to convince my friends of this fact.

I told them repeatedly that they must not regard me as being insane, and used all my powers of persuasion to induce them to believe that I was not demented, but only in ill health. But they retorted that the air and manner I adopted in my endeavors to dissuade them from their belief in my insanity showed conclusively that I was no longer capable of

intelligently regulating and governing my conduct or
general deportment, and indeed confirmed them, if
confirmation were needed, in their belief.

Meeting with such poor success here, I next turned
my attention to Dr. Wallace, and endeavored to convince *him* that my mind was unimpaired. I expostu-
lated with him, and inveighed against the manifest
injustice of confining a sane man as a lunatic, etc.,
with much more to the same purpose. But instead
of all this having the effect so greatly desired, its
results were directly contrary, and convinced Dr.
Wallace (the Superintendent of the asylum) that my
case was more hopeless than he had supposed. Hence
I came to the sincere and not unnatural, though perhaps extravagant, conclusion that Dr. Wallace, my
family and my friends, were all insane! and I wondered that the general public had not long ago discovered this fact. However, this being the case, I
could not blame them for incarcerating me, for this
fact was sufficient evidence that they were sincere in
believing me insane. But, after reflecting over the
matter for a long time, I began to be haunted by the
fear that they might not be content with merely con-
signing me to the asylum, but might *take my life!*

This fear finally assumed large proportions, and I
saw no prospect, even the most remote, of release,
hence my life at the asylum was more bitter than
death. The slow years passed away, and still they
kept me a close prisoner, constantly watched and
guarded, and the great desire of my heart for freedom
was no nearer its acccomplishment. Yet in all this

time my mind no doubt had improved, while there was no denying the fact that muscular and bodily vigor were certainly very much increased under the skillful and rational treatment of Drs. Wallace and White. Yet (if the truth must be told) I must say that it was very much against my will that I took any medicine at all, because I feared that they might be plotting against my life. Now, looking back over those unhappy years, I cannot find it in my heart to regret them. Dark as they were, and full of gloom, they no doubt served a useful purpose, and I can recall them every one without rancor of heart or bitterness of spirit.

But having reached the conclusion that the authorities would never release me, and being fully determined to remain no longer than I could help, there was but one course left to me, and that was to escape. This was accordingly resolved upon. How or when to accomplish this desideratum—how to begin, and how proceed—I did not know. But this much I *did* know: That however doubtful might be my chances for escape, and the exact manner of going about it, there was no uncertainty in my mind with reference to my resolution to escape. This determination was unfaltering and invincible. The manner of its accomplishment, however, was a source of much perplexity to me for a great while, and much time was spent in an endeavor to contrive a plan which should promise some hope of success. But there were so many difficulties in the way that they seemed insuperable.

I had read of wonderful escapes from the terrible
dungeons of historic prisons, on both sides of the
Atlantic, and I even thought of the celebrated Chateau
D'If; but none of these would apply to the present
case, and it should seem that I was doomed to puzzle
myself in vain.   At night we were locked in our cells
from the outside, and it was not possible to leave
them until the keeper saw fit to unlock the door.   It
was therefore manifestly impossible to escape at
night, or even to leave my cell.   Truly, as long as
they had me locked in for the night, the only escape
I could ever hope to make would begin and end in
my imagination merely.   During the day-time we
could walk about the grounds—under a guard—as
much as we pleased—provided always that we did
not please to walk too much or too far.   But had I
been able to overpower the guard—which was a feat
not to be thought of for a moment—I should not have
been a great deal better off than before. The grounds
were inclosed by a stout plank wall some fourteen feet
in height, and upon this, two steel barbed wires were
tightly and firmly stretched (for the express purpose
of foiling such attempts as the one I had then in con-
templation).   This wall was very strong, and was
always kept in good repair.   There was not a crack
or break in it large enough to admit a humming-bird.
Nothing in truth but a heavy axe in well-trained
hands would demolish it; and even admitting that
I could procure the latter implement at the proper
time—and this of course was out of the question—the
unavoidable noise occasioned by the work of destroy-

ing the wall would bring out the whole establishment upon me.

Thus it will be seen how slender and precarious were my hopes of escape—how doubtful it seemed that I should ever be able to leave the hated precincts of the asylum—how probable it appeared that my stay there would prove to be indefinite,—or which indeed would run up into a term of years of which I shuddered to think.

Yet in spite of all this; in spite of their care, and of the fact that I was under almost constant watch and ward; I was ultimately enabled to bid defiance to cells, guards, and steel-plated walls, and to make my escape. Notwithstanding all the plans which I had so carefully laid from time to time for this purpose, none of them seemed feasible, or ever materialized; and thus it chanced that when I finally made my escape, the plan by which I accomplished it was wholly the result of an accident, occurring in an unexpected way and at an unlooked-for time, and was taken advantage of upon the spur of the moment. Happily, it proved successful, as the reader shall see.

Thus, many of the most important actions of our lives turn upon points comparatively trivial within themselves; and we little think, when some small and apparently insignificant accident impels us to adopt an unexpected course of action, that in all human probability we are doing that which may entirely change the social and moral tenor of our future.

I think it was first in the spring or summer of the year 1888 that the asylum authorities, realizing that

many lunatics were happier and more contented when
employed at some light manual labor, and feeling
the urgent need of some means by which such employment could be given them, established a hospital
farm to be worked by alternate parties of lunatics.
Many of the inmates to whom the farm labor was
thus assigned went about their task in a cheerful and
even eager spirit, and were often to be heard whist-
ling or singing with great complacency, or in other
ways manifesting a more buoyant and hopeful turn
of mind.   But there were others who looked upon
all manual labor, even the lightest, with great aver-
sion, and no amount of argument or persuasion could
ever induce them to believe it in any way desirable
or helpful to them.   Whether compulsory measures
were ever directed against the latter class I cannot
now remember; but I heard them at times, while
walking in the park, cursing and swearing at the
authorities for making "farm-hands" out of them.
While I did not have much faith in anything they
said, either one way or another (for there are among
maniacs, as well as elsewhere, men who are not over-
scrupulous in their adherence to truth) I must say
that any outsider who had chanced to overhear their
diatribes would certainly have supposed that they
had been commanded at the muzzle of a gun to sur-
render their honor and their lives, at the very least.

   The workers were roused at an early hour in the
morning, partook of a hasty breakfast, and were
marched under guard to the farm.   Every morning
about two hours before the break of day, a keeper

visited the cells of those who were detailed to labor that day, unlocked the doors, shouted at the sleeping lunatic until he answered, and, the round being finished, and the requisite number awakened, he returned to his bed. It was rare indeed that any one of the laborers had to be awakened a second time. Generally the unlocking of their doors broke the spell woven by their slumbers, and they turned out of bed immediately, and were soon at their post. Such was the discipline maintained, and the wholesome fear it inspired, that there was scarcely a man in the entire precincts of the asylum who would have disobeyed an order or willfully violated a rule. Hence on being awakened they promptly dressed themselves and assembled 'near the dining-room.

One morning in the fall of the year 1888 an attendant came round as usual to wake the laborers. By some mistake—for he was a new hand, having been employed but the day before—he came to my cell, unlocked the door, called to me, and told me to get up. He then went on his rounds, and I have never seen him from that day to this. I knew in a moment that he had made a mistake, and I lay in perfect silence for some moments wondering at the circumstance. But the cell door stood most invitingly open, and I saw that it was yet quite dark. Then a wild thought struck me with sudden force:

"Was it possible that I could make practical use of the keeper's error in any way?"

I hardly dared to allow the thought that came rushing upon me to assume more definite proportions or shape itself into words. Trembling betwixt fear and excitement, I sat up in my narrow bed, and threw back the scanty covering. Then without allowing myself further time for reflection, I rose hastily and dressed myself. Vaguely and almost unconsciously the desire, as well as the resolve to escape—or at least to make the attempt—was shaping itself in my mind.

I pulled my door open and cautiously peeped out. It was hardly light enough, however, to see anything, and I boldly stepped out into the dark obscurity of the corridor and slowly and circumspectly groped my way down stairs. I knew that it was not possible for me to leave the building unless I went out with the field-hands, as every egress was securely locked; and I knew that whenever I showed my face to the guard in charge of the laborers that they would recognize me and lock me again in my cell.

For some minutes I stood at the bottom of the stairway in anxious thought, turning over in my mind the probable chances for and against my escape, and endeavoring to evolve some plan more promising than the one presented to me. I did not care to make an attempt which was more than likely to prove self-abortive, knowing that it would only subject me to greater hardships, and frustrate any future chances I might have of a like nature. But the longer I meditated, the more determined I grew and, the calmer and more self-possessed I became. The sound of clattering dishes, and the movements of men at table, came up to me from the kitchen below,

together with the appetizing odor of coffee and broil-
ing ham. But the tumult of thoughts within me drove
back for the moment all baser appetites, and I
thought only of the resolution to escape that was
fixing itself unalterably in my mind.

Presently the noise of rattling dishes ceased. I
heard some orders given in a sharp imperious voice,
and the group of lunatics filed out of the breakfast
room. The foremost of them passed the spot where
I stood, hidden in the shadow, and I shrank further
back into the darkness. I observed, however, that
the guards having already gone by the stairway where
I was concealed, were walking in front with their
lanterns, and the lunatics marching after them.
Then with a wild throb of hope I remembered that
often it was only at the big entrance-gates that the
head guard inspected each face by the light from his
lantern as its owner passed out. This led me to believe that perhaps the file of lunatics (and by taking
three steps, I could make myself one of them), might
not be inspected very closely at the outer door of
the main building, and I might therefore be lucky
enough to get out into the grounds. What I should
do in the latter case was a contingency I did not
stop to puzzle over. I only knew that although I
could not leave the grounds through the customary
egresses without permission, (which would never be
given) I could at least have the satisfaction of making
a determined endeavor to do so. I therefore instantly
resolved to take my place among the laborers, trusting to the darkness to pass unrecognized.

This resolution was no sooner formed than I stepped quietly forward as the last of the farm-hands passed me, and walked along with them, but among the hindermost. None of them observed me or seemed to be aware of the fact that anyone had joined them, neither did any of them look back. They preferred— with the superstitious cowardice of a child—to keep their eyes upon the light in front rather than gaze about them at the surrounding darkness, or run the chance (to them a serious one) of seeing suspicious shadows lurking in dark corners. Hence no one observed me.

A short turn brought us into the main hall, and a few moments later we heard the great bolts click, and the outer doors swing back. With a beating heart, but with a mind fully resolved, I kept my place among my companions, and we neared the door where, accordingly as I was stopped or permitted to pass, hung the failure or success of my attempt. Would it, I found myself wondering, prove to be merely an *attempt*, or a successful escape—a coup d'état? The cool fresh air of early morning poured into the hall, grateful and sweet. I heard the gentle soughing of the breeze outside, and the distant sound of closing doors.

Two of the guards were standing carelessly conversing upon the ground just outside, but the head guard inside the hall stood not far from the door with his lantern in his hand. Those in the van passed out, the keeper paying very little attention to any of them. *Tramp! tramp!* the steady feet marched over the floor, and the last few laborers, of whom I was one, were opposite the guard and almost upon the threshold of the door. My eyes were fixed upon the keeper in the deepest anxiety, but he was looking another way. Thank heaven! the door is reached!.... but hold! Turning suddenly and without a moment's warning, the guard directs his gaze towards us. It seems to me that his eyes are fixed keenly upon my face. He steps toward us, raising his lantern as he comes. My heart gives a great bound and almost stands still, but I am determined to face whatever comes with a bold front. One instant of dreadful suspense, and the guard stops... beside a lunatic several feet ahead of me, and flashes his light in his face, but says nothing. Apparently satisfied, he grunts, lowers his lantern, steps back, and orders us to hurry. The reaction of feeling is so great that for a moment I feel dizzy and faint, but—the door is passed, and I find myself walking under the wide canopy of heaven — not free, but about to become so.

It yet wanted some two hours of day, and everything was obscured in the gray darkness of early morning. A damp breeze came from the south, and the sky was rendered murky and threatening by the presence of ominous-looking clouds. We filed off down the graveled walk, but I knew that I must contrive to slip away from my companions, or be detected at the entrance-gates and sent ignominiously back to my cell.

It seems strange to me now, in thinking of this incident, that no guard was placed behind us that morning. It was so dark that it would have been a comparatively easy matter for anyone, two, or even three of the laborers to have stolen away from their fellows in the darkness without much fear of detection. They could not, I suppose, have escaped from the premises, and they would probably have been taken again almost immediately; but it would have occasioned the guards no little trouble and uneasiness, and such an occurrence could have been effectually prevented by the simple expedient of placing a keeper or two in the rear with their lanterns. As a matter of fact, I shall always be thankful that they did not do so. Their indifference (call it what you will) on that morning doubtless assisted me no little in making my escape, for which I have already said I am thankful, and so I am; yet I wonder at their negligence.

My companions up to this point had never appeared to notice my presence among them. In the darkness therefore, and when it was not easy to distinguish faces, the only light being that afforded by the lanterns which were born in front, I fell back somewhat. Then, watching my chance, and when I thought no one was looking, I sprang off the walk into the darkness. In an instant, almost, I was safely hidden in the profusion of shrubbery which abounded in that part of the grounds. From this retreat I watched the onward progress of the column of dark figures with a variety of emotions. In fancy I could almost hear the alarmed shouts of the guard, the order to halt, the command for an instant and vigorous search, and for the sounding of a general alarm.

But nothing of the kind took place. All was silent
save for the noise of the marching feet of the field-
hands. No one had appeared to miss me, and the
guards themselves believed me to be locked securely
in my cell. I stood for some minutes listening to
their steady tramp, and the noisy opening and shutting
of the gates. Their dark forms had every moment
grown vaguer and dimmer, and now the sound of
their footsteps became more indistinct and finally
died away in the distance, the lanterns in the van
glimmering and bobbing up and down until they also
were lost to view. Then all was still.

I left my hiding-place and looked about me. Slim
evergreen shrubs stood at intervals about the grounds,
looking like motionless sentinels at their posts. The
gatekeeper's cottage in one corner was a mere heap
of undefined blackness; and my gaze traveling thence
rested upon the steel-crowned walls of the park. I
gazed upon it—or rather upon its black outlines—
with a feeling of more intense hate than I had ever
felt before towards any object of inanimate nature.
Almost in imagination I could see the silent figures
of the lunatics as they wandered ceaselessly up and
down, the pallid ghosts of their slumbering selves.
"Ah!" thought I, "it is for the last time, in very truth,
hated park, that I shall gaze upon your sombre outlines! Then let me bear with me in my wanderings
every hated detail of your appearance." And though
the night was too dark for me to see aught of it but
the environing wall, yet I knew that already its de-
spised outlines were so impressed upon the tablets of

my brain that neither time nor tide could eradicate
them. Even had I at the moment been stricken
blind, still I felt that wherever I turned I should behold the fatal outlines of that park, haunting me like
an ominous ghost. Turning my back upon it now,
I saw the asylum building rising before me in the
darkness, grim, black and threatening. With a shudder, I turned from that also, and went towards the
wall I had yet to scale. I realized that my task had
just begun, and that when daylight broke it must find
me far away. The time left me was very short, yet
ere it passed, it was necessary to the further progress
of my escape that I should find some means of getting
out of the asylum grounds.

These and other thoughts were occupying my mind
as I went towards the fence. I kept as far from the
graveled walk as possible; for although I knew that
no one about the premises was astir, with the possible
exception of the cook, I feared that by some chance
the sound of my feet crunching upon the gravel might
be heard, and an investigation, fatal to my hopes,
should follow. The wall was built of heavy, solid,
pine boards, and the two lines of barbed wire were
fastened securely upon the top. How could I ever
scale a perpendicular wall fifteen feet in height?
How balance myself upon the top? There was
absolutely nothing to hold to, or with which to support myself for a moment after I had mounted it. I
thought of these difficulties as I approached it, and
could presently see its black outlines rising before
me. It seemed hopelessly tall, strong, and impreg-

nable as I stood beneath it. I remained for some moments turning over in my mind various plans and projects for surmounting the obstacle which threatened to wreck my hopes of escape even before I had fairly begun it.

Then by good fortune I remembered seeing a plank somewhere in the grounds the day before. I turned back in the darkness to seek it. Round and round, back and forth I went, somtimes crawling on my hands, feeling my way in the gloom. Presently my hand struck against something hard and firm. My search was ended. I had found the board. I examined it as carefully as was possible under the circumstances, and found that it would probably hold my weight; but it had been warped by long exposure to the sun and wind, and was crooked and rickety. I judged its length to be about twelve feet—perhaps a little more. Yet no bit of rosewood or mahogany was ever as welcome as that warped pine board was to me, for it meant freedom. Throwing it upon my shoulder I went back joyfully to the wall and placed it in position. A new difficulty, however, now arose. I was wearing the asylum uniform, and it lacked much of being in a good state of repair. I knew that the sharp barbs of the wire above would badly damage if not entirely ruin it. And as I had no means of procuring another suit, I had no choice but protect the one I had. My pockets were entirely empty. I had not so much as a cent of money, or even a pen-knife. It took me but a moment to decide as to the best means of preserving my clothes. Hastily, but

carefully, I removed them, made them into a knot with
a brick in the center to give the bundle weight, and
cast it over the fence.   Hearing it fall safely on the
other side, I placed myself upon the plank and began
to crawl up.   It was a slow and tedious business, drag-
ging myself painfnlly over the rough surface of the old
board, rickety as it was, and with its precarious support, and I came near falling back repeatedly.   But
I accomplished it at last, and found myself clinging
to the dizzy top of the wall.   It was next to impossible for me to balance myself, and I had no other
resource but to kick my plank away and fall rather
than jump to the ground below.   This I did.   Giving
it a shove with my foot I sent it crashing to the earth;
then turning my hold loose, I fell headlong to the
ground below, expecting to break a leg at the very
least.   But as my good fortune would have it, I
dropped directly upon the bundle of clothing, and thus
had the force of my fall so much broken that I did
not experience any unpleasant effects except the
sudden shock.   Scrambling hurriedly to my feet, I
resumed the cast-off clothing and looked about me.
It had grown something lighter and day would break
in less than an hour.   Dark threatening clouds still
scurried across the sky, or hung ominously athwart
the face of the heavens.   The damp wind from the
south no longer blew, and it seemed to me that fogs
and mists were rising.   Altogether it presaged a
rainy day, and the deep silence of early dawn rested
over all.

    With a shudder I turned away, feeling a strange

depression, but never dreaming that my trials, hard though they had been to bear, were not yet begun, and that there were innumerable thrilling adventures and terrible privations that I had still to endure.

So in the leaden gray of early morning I turned my back upon the North Texas Insane Asylum, well knowing that in a few short hours hue and cry would be raised after me, persistent search made, and the telegraph set in motion. But though alone, without money, and afraid to communicate with my relatives, I resolved to outwit them, for I did not intend ever to be taken captive.

CHAPTER III.

Misfortune brings
Sorrow enough; 'tis envy to ourselves
To augment it by perdition.

Habbington.

With the object of filling up an awkward gap that
would otherwise occur at this point, and that the
successive chapters may have the interest and con-
tinuity of a regular narrative, a brief account is here
given of the events which occurred immediately after
Mr. Fleming's escape from the asylum, and up to the
time when he was first heard from.

Late in the autumn of the year 1888 a message was
sent to the family of Mr. E. B. Fleming announcing
the fact that he had made his escape in some mysterious manner from the asylum, and that no trace of
him could be found. A vigorous search was at once
instituted, and inquiries made in every direction, but
all to no purpose. The asylum authörities could not
learn, and do not know to this day, in what manner
he made his escape, or in what direction he went.
He had vanished as utterly as though the earth had
opened and swallowed him, leaving no sign or clew
behind him. He was therefore given up for dead,
as it was known that he had been very despondent

72

and had made attempts upon his own life. Accordingly, the only solution of the profound mystery attending his escape and disappearance was the supposition that he had drowned himself, and he was thenceforward mourned as one dead.

This side of the story got abroad, and all who had known him in former years came to believe that his life had drawn to its close in the dark depths of some unknown lagoon. Men whispered among themselves of the blighted life and melancholy ending of one whom they had known as the incarnation of energy and thrift; and this sad story was given wide circulation.

Meanwhile time passed on, and his family had long since given up all hope of ever finding the slightest clew as to the exact manner of his death. But one day some years after a letter came from an old family servant from whom nothing had been heard in many years—a faithful negro named Dick, who, after having married a termagant of a mulatto, had left the service of the family and degenerated into a ragged loafer about town. The letter was post-marked at San Antonio, Texas, and, as near as it could be made out, for every word was spelled in a manner wholly original with the writer, and quite unheard-of before, while the penmanship might have passed for a rude map of the holy land, went on to state after a long preamble that the writer had just returned from Mexico; that during his absence he had seen one of Mrs Fleming's *particular friends*, who had inquired about the family; but that the writer could give him

no information as to whether they were dead or alive,
not having heard from them in many years. Whereupon, the black letter-writer, after offering a rambling
apology for writing to his "ole mistress" at all, prayed
that she would, if living, give him such information
as she thought would satisfy the friendly curiosity of
an old acquaintance. After this, commending her to
the mercy of God in very bad English, and assuring
her, in worse English, that he was now religious, as
she *ought* to be, the letter closed.

Having no suspicion whatever as to the identity of
this friend, an immediate answer was nevertheless
returned to the garrulous old negro, containing the
information asked for. Sometime after this elapsed
before anything more was heard from him; but, after
a long delay, a shorter letter came from the same
place, acknowledging the receipt of the letter from
his "ole mistress." He apologized for his unaccountable procrastination, and thanked her for her
condescension in noticing his unsolicited communication at all. He stated that her "friend" was satisfied
and pleased with the intelligence he had been, through
her courtesy, enabled to convey to him. Alluding
in mysterious term to some "dear one," whom he did
not even remotely name, nor mention what relation-
ship existed between her or him and the "friend," and
also of the strange fate which permitted some persons
to rise as from the dead, but neglecting to state just
how this applied to Mr. Fleming's family, he brought
his second letter to a close.

From this time on letters came now and then from

various persons who had known the family in former years, and it was astonishing to see how great a variety of trades, men and things were represented in the person of these many letter-writers. There were letters from old negro servants, from farm hands, from brick-masons, from lawyers, from merchants, from real estate dealers, from tobacconists, and so on through half the gamut of avocations, trades and professions. Many indeed came from men whom the family had never so much as heard of, and almost always asking for "information" of every conceivable kind, or for copies of the local newspapers. But however the different constituents of this epistolary avalanche differed from each other in the main, they had one point in common, and all, without exception contained vague allusions to a "friend" of the family. The reader need hardly be told how tantalizing all this finally became. However, the constant and almost periodical recurrence of these indefinite hints soon awakened a suspicion in the minds of the family that possibly, by some strange chance, this "friend" so often alluded to, might have seen Mr. Fleming himself since his disappearance from the asylum. The last of these strange communications came from a real estate dealer in the city of San Diego, California, and he was at once appealed to to give the family any information that might be of interest to them. The request was purposely put in these vague terms in order to allow the gentleman as much latitude as possible. This gentleman's name was Mr. James N. Cook, and the appeal was not made to him in vain.   His generous nature was touched, and he responded   at once, confessing that not only had the "friend" so frequently mentioned actually seen Mr. Fleming,   but that the "friend" was none other than Mr. Fleming himself.

He then went on to say that the latter was at that time residing in San Diego, and had lived in California for something near two years; that he had fully recovered his health and spirits, and was as sound mentally as he had ever been.   The rejoicing occa- .
sioned by this intelligence had hardly subsided when the family received a letter from Mr. Fleming himself, and an immediate correspondence ensued   A few months later he returned to his home; but little the worse for his strange and romantic experiences.

CHAPTER IV.

Through the shadowy past,
Like a tomb-searcher, Memory ran,
Lifting each shroud that Time had cast
O'er buried hopes.   *Moore.*

Not a great distance from the asylum building, ran a small stream. Its banks on either side are pretty thickly wooded, and altogether it is a secluded spot. Turning my face east on leaving the hospital grounds in the early gray of that autumn morning, I directed my steps towards this stream, hoping to bewilder my pursuers in the mazes of the copse. After traveling in this direction for perhaps a quarter of a mile, I turn-ed off north for a few hundred yards, then west, and finally east again, "doubling" on my tracks a good part of the way. After reaching the wood I pur-posely wound about in various directions, wading in the stream at times, and "doubling" on my tracks.

Then for the third time setting my face east, I emerged from the woodland, with the intention of getting to the railroad and following it for a time. By some strange freak of fortune I struck my foot against some object which lay in my pathway, and on picking it up found it to be a good riding-bridle

77

of black leather, and which was almost new. I felt
this to be a God-send, as it did not seem to me likely
that anyone would ever think of apprehending a man
in search of a horse which had escaped from him
while his owner was engaged in Bacchanalian revels.
At least I meant to leave this impression on anyone whom I might chance to meet. While on the
other hand, a man wandering about with no good
excuse for his circumforanean proclivities (for my
personal appearance might have caused me to be
taken for a professional itinerant) might excite a
suspicion that should be fatal to his hopes. And I
may here say that one secret of my unusual success
in evading detection was to be found in the fact that
I was at all times able to give a satisfactory account
of myself. Always beforehand I had a carefully prepared excuse to pass myself on without detention.

Striking out resolutely east, with the bridle upon
my arm, I walked at an even but rapid pace. Day
was now breaking, and I realized the necessity of
haste. In my onward progress I encountered several
individuals before the sun rose, but I always abated
my speed as I neared them. The first one I met was
an elderly gentleman coming slowly along near the
railroad. I observed that he looked at me a little
curiously, hence I did not give him time to become
suspicious. I boldly approached him and inquired if
he had seen "a riderless horse with a saddle on, but
no bridle, anywhere that morning." He paused,
bent his head in evident thought for a moment, and
then told me that he had not.

Having thus answered my question very civilly, he asked, with some appearance of curiosity:

"What is the matter?"

"Nothing," I replied, "except that I took a little too much 'tea' with the boys at Terrell last night, and my horse has escaped from me."

I then proceeded to say to the stranger, in the hope of giving my story greater probability, that I would pay a reward of $25 for the return of my animal to Canton. He thereupon took out a note-book, and asked me to describe my horse. I answered without hesitation that he was a large, powerfully-built roan, with a bald face and two white feet. When my inquisitive friend had noted this description down, I bade him good-bye and hastened on my way. He called after me before I had gone a great distance to say that he would send a man out instantly to search for my runaway.

Further down the road I met a fat negress waddling along the highway to whom I put the same formula. Fixing her dull eyes shrewdly upon my face, as soon as I had spoken, and placing her pudgy arms akimbo, she answered in the glibest manner imaginable that she had seen such a horse not far away, only a few minutes since; that she had endeavored to catch him, but that he had shaken his heels in the air and run off into a neighboring wood. I would find him, she continued, *up there* about half a mile away. The reader will no doubt understand that I was very greatly surprised to learn that my horse was so near at hand. I knew, however, that the fat wench was deliberately lying in the hope of getting a reward for her mendacity. But I had nothing to give her, or I should have given her a small piece of silver. I left her standing in the middle of the road gazing after me with an expression made up of the extremes of astonishment, anger and disappointed virtue.

The sun was now rising, hence I was under the necessity of exercising special care to avoid all human habitations; yet, whenever my eye fell upon the homelike vision of smoke rising from near-by chimneys, and I knew that some housewife was busily preparing the morning meal, I looked at it longingly, for I had had no breakfast and was growing hungry. But no time could now be spared for this or like purposes, my only object being to put as great a distance as was possible that day between the asylum and myself. Therefore I doubled my speed after losing sight of the negress, sometimes walking and again trotting over the lonely roads I was following. In this manner I continued all the morning, hardly giving myself a moment's rest, but keeping, nevertheless, all my senses upon the alert. The rapid walking became very fatiguing, but an iron-barred cell was behind me and freedom in front, and I did not spare myself. I did not know at the time—nor indeed until long afterwards—that for some reason I was not missed until nearly night, and that I therefore had a full day's start. But not knowing this I traveled all day at the top of my speed, and was afraid even to stop to get my breath.

In four hours after leaving the outskirts of Terrell
I reached Will's Point, near twenty miles away,
having walked that distance in a little less than three
and a half hours. I made a wide *détour* around the
town, without stopping, and held on my way. The
bridle that I had found near Terrell I kept for some
time and threw away. The threatening clouds that
in the early morning had hung over the sky had
passed away without fulfilling their prophecy of rain.
The day that succeeded was one of those bright clear
days for which the autumn season is so renowned in
song and story; when a celestial peace—a brooding
calm, sleeps over the wide face of nature, and the
blue serene of heaven.

But little of this lay on my mind that memorable
day. Exulting in the happy sense of freedom, yet
pursued by haunting cares, and a comparative feeling
of helplessness, I had thoughts only for the means
by which escape might be best facilitated, and capture
rendered uncertain or improbable. For I realized
that my only safety lay in flight.

And now about this time a strange phenomenon
began to manifest itself—one that I do not remember
ever to have heard or read of. My memory for a time
in some respects had been befogged and obscured to
that extent that many incidents of the past had passed
wholly from my recollection, and I could never recall
them, even for a moment.

I had observed, however, that within a few hours
after my escape the scenes and incidents so long forgotten began to crowd upon me,—and this not as

the mere mechanical recurrence of disconnected
recollections, as one thing and another called them
up, but in a vast procession of vivid and distinct
pictures, beginning with early childhood and advanc-
ing step by step to the period when my mind first
lost its equipoise.   It was a solemn and mournful
pageant, sweeping in continuous procession before
my mind—an almost illimitable array of joy and
pleasure, and sorrow and woe.   Faces that the mists
of time had long ago obscured or wholly blotted out;
voices now stilled in death; incidents whose actors
had been mouldering in the grave for five-and-twenty
years; scenes that in a former day had been of passing interest; pictures of long forgotten acts and deeds;
sad memories of home and of childhood, and of my
mother;—all these came in a mighty succession before me.   Nor did they come in one jumbled and
confused mass, indistinct and chaotic; but picture
by picture, scene by scene, like living reality.   It
was a vast and endless panorama, projected upon a
measureless screen by some mighty invisible magic
lantern, with all the pomp and brilliant show which
awakened imagination could lend to it.   Whole pages
that I had read came before me, just as they had
appeared in the printed book, but with a vivid and
lurid brightness that was as startling as it was unaccountable.   It seemed to me that some mighty and
devouring light shone from within, its vivifying rays
falling upon the hidden springs of memory and rousing them to phenomenal action.   And there was the
memory of one voice, which, though forgotten for

many years, now came rolling through the intervening mists of time and struck upon some hidden chord
that vibrated beneath its touch. This voice I knew
had long been stilled in death;—its very memory had
ceased to be; but, as if hallowed and grown sacred
by the swift rush of years, it came over me now,
bringing with it the songs it had sung, the words it
had uttered, chastened by time and sorrow and the
purifying fires of affliction. The sweet airs that it
had sung for me in the faraway past swept over me
with a cadence exquisitely mournful and solemn,
transporting me back to scenes whose memory yet
remained, surviving the vicissitudes of life, the
mutations of fortune, and of time and tide.

And stranger still, grand and harmonious strains
of music and supernal symphonies, came now and
then to my ears, soul-stirring and faint; now dying
away into immeasurable distance and now swelling,
sublime and mournful, into unknown airs and heavenly
harmonies. And it seemed to me, as each mysterious
strain came on the breeze, that sobs of unspeakable
anguish, as from an eternity of woe, burst with heart-
quaking intensity from the lips of the invisible
musicians.

Pleasant although all this may have been at first,
it soon became a source of continual annoyance to
me, as well as uneasiness; nor did I feel wholly safe
and free from alarm until this remarkable condition
had passed away. After worrying and perplexing
me for several days, it at length disappeared, leaving
my mind brighter than it had been for three years,

and it was then that I began to realize for the first time that my mind had been affected. Yet I felt how vain it would be to hope to convince the asylum authorities or my friends that my mental equilibrium had been restored, or almost so. (For had I not maintained all along that it had never been disturbed?) Hence, remembering these things now, I renewed my determination to keep my fate a profound secret from all who had ever known me.

Between the hours of one and two o'clock P. M, I reached the village of Canton—a distance of thirty-one and a half miles from Terrell. All that afternoon I walked steadily and unceasingly, so that by sunset I found that I had traveled since leaving the asylum a distance of *five-and forty miles*. This statement may appear like an endeavor to draw the long bow, as the proverb-maker puts it, and the more so when it is remembered that I had been for so long a time confined without any active exercise, but it is nevertheless true. Yet the mighty effort required to make this long distance, and the intense nervous excitement which urged me forward, came near prostrating me —so much so, indeed, that for some days thereafter I crept along at a snail's pace, hardly averaging a score of miles *per diem* of ten hours.

Shortly after sunset I came to a home-like farmhouse on the side of the road, and stopped to inquire if they could give me lodging for the night. They told me that they could not; but that not a great distance away I would find the home of a gentleman whose family was visiting at a distance, and who

therefore had the house to himself. As a consequence, they went on to say, he would no doubt be
glad of my company until the morrow. I thanked
them for their kindness and hurried off down a dim
"neighborhood road" which was pointed out to me,
and in the gray dusk of early evening found myself
standing before a large old-fashioned homestead with
a great many trees in the yard. As I neared the
gate, several large hounds ran barking to the fence,
but at a command from their master, who now appeared in the doorway, they crept sullenly under the
house. The master then came out to the gate and
invited me to come in. I told him that I had been
referred to him by some ladies, who had spoken of
him in a very complimentary manner, and that I was
in search of some place at which to spend the night,
but that I did not have any money.

He replied to me very kindly, asked me to come in,
and told me that I was welcome. I accepted this
friendly invitation gratefully, and we entered the house
together. Supper was then on the table, and we sat
down to it. I had had nothing whatever in the way
of food for four-and-twenty hours, and felt weak and
faint. Yet my repast was a very light one, as I had
appetite for very little. I partook of his good cheer
so sparingly that my host, before whose assaults the
various dishes were disappearing with marvelous
celerity, inquired whether the supper suited me. I
satisfied him by replying that I was ill, and this was
the exact truth. We then rose from the table and
returned to the sitting-room, where a number of fine

hounds lay stretched before the fire. Some fishing-tackle lay on one of the beds, and the walls were liberally furnished with pictures of a sporting character. Cartridge-belts and game-bags were distributed about in the most astonishing positions, while one corner was devoted to an assortment of guns. Obviously my worthy host was of a sporting turn, and our conversation ran largely upon such matters, in all of which I duly displayed the densest ignorance. My entertainer, delighted at finding some one who would patiently listen to his interminable harangues upon what to him was the topic of all topics, spent the next two hours in expatiating gleefully and at great length upon these questions, going into the minutest details, and fairly "talking me deaf," for I heard not a word he said. Finally I escaped by excusing myself on the score of fatigue, and was shown to my room.

One would naturally suppose that after having walked a distance of five-and-forty miles between sunrise and sunset, I should have sunk into a profound slumber on retiring to bed. Yet such was not the case. The absolute silence and stillness which reigned around me were opressive. The wild shrieks and shrill howls which had sounded in my ears night after night for three long years had accomplished their work, and I found it impossible to sleep. The deep stillness which prevailed became ominous and awe-inspiring from its very profoundness, and disturbed me as no noise could have done. If some unearthly voice had shrieked and howled in my ears for an hour or two, I should have slept sweetly the whole night through; but as it was I felt far more exhausted and depressed when the long night ended than when it begun.

My host called me a full hour before day, and I rose and went out to breakfast with him. He remarked upon my pallid face and heavy eyes, and I told him I had not rested well. Breakfast being ended, I thanked him in appropriate terms for his courtesy, and bidding him farewell I went on my way.

The day before, on leaving Canton, I had traveled south until evening; but on this morning I turned east again. Physical weakness troubled me to-day. I traveled along at a steady swinging walk, but was tormented by a sense of weakness and exhaustion that made me uneasy, as I feared my strength might fail. Again, the visions brought forward by my awakened memory worried and annoyed me. But towards evening this state of my mind began to pass away, and remarkable as it may seem, my strength began to return, and the tormenting sense of weakness to leave me.

I did not stop anywhere for dinner, but went without it, preferring to do this rather than lose the time, and for other reasons. I passed the night at a farmhouse some twenty miles from my first stop. Rousing me up at an early hour the next morning, the lady of the house gave me a lunch as soon as I had partaken of breakfast, and sent me on my way.

On this morning I felt somewhat better than the

day before, and found myself in better condition for travel. Yet I had slept but little, and had passed most of the night in tossing on my bed. Towards night I passed through the city of Tyler—a place famous all over the State for the beauty and grace of its women, and the wealth and enterprise of its citizens. Some hours later in the day the road I followed led me in a more desolate and uninhabited part of the country than any I had yet traveled. Near night indeed the face of the earth became wild, lonely and unbroken by human habitations, and I began to fear that I should have no place to pass the night except upon the greensward. This thought was far from being a comfortable one, as the route I was traversing led through a large and lonely forest, and I had no means of self-defense against prowling beasts, or even an overcoat to shelter me from the chill air of night.

I had passed the last farm-house some hours before, and had seen no person or indication of human presence since. The sun had already sunk; and in the deep solitudes and shadows of the forest, night was rapidly closing in. I may be pardoned for the slight feeling of uneasiness which possessed me. The prospect of a night spent in the forest, with no bed but the earth and no covering but the sky, was anything but inviting, and I hurried on, pausing now and then and listening, in the endeavor to catch any sounds which might indicate the proximity of human beings. But none could be heard, and I was upon the point of turning aside to seek a sheltered resting-place for the night while there was yet some vestige of daylight remaining upon the rapidly darkening earth, when, in rounding a sudden curve in the road, I caught the welcome gleam of light. Apparently it came from a small building off to the right of the highway, darkly outlined upon the forest behind, and a dim bridle path appeared to lead up to it. Guided by the gleam and flicker of the light, I made my way to the door of the small structure. At my knock a high cracked voice called out, as if in much surprise: "Whose dar?"

Then steps were heard; the door swung open on loudly-creaking hinges; and the dark form of an aged negro confronted me, his black shadow grotesquely marked upon the ground in front by the light which escaped from the open doorway. Without waiting for him to begin, for his shadow fell upon me and rendered the color of my skin a matter of doubt to his age-bedimmed eyes, I stated my dilemma in the fewest and plainest words. As soon as he was made to understand that a white man stood before him, he doffed his ragged hat, bowed low, and bade me enter. The interior of the cabin was fully in keeping with what I could see of the exterior. The unmistakable signs of the most abject poverty were everywhere apparent, and the walls were black and smoke-stained. The shanty itself was rickety and quivered beneath our tread; the walls were full of cracks through which the chill autumn air came in unimpeded currents. The light was supplied by a small dingy oil lamp, its blaze flickering and spluttering under the currents of air which swept over it, as it rested upon a weather beaten pie box, and by a huge log fire which crackcled merrily on the hearth. The furniture was of the rudest and most meagre description, consisting, so far as I could see, of two pine-bottomed and crazy chairs, several empty soap boxes, a few cooking utensils, and a pair of black greasy blankets thrown carelessly into a corner. I concluded that the latter were made to serve as both bed and blankets, as neither mattress nor bedstead was visible. In another corner a quantity of fresh cotton seed, with an unnecessary amount of lint still adhering, had been thrown, probably also to serve as a bed in an emergency.

The old negro, whose wool was snowy white, and whose wrinkled hands trembled with the infirmity of age, invited me, with the old-fashioned politeness of the venerable family slave, to "take a chair and be seated." He then informed me, with much wordy circumlocution, and in the grotesque and inimitable dialect of his race, that I should probably have to remain with him over night, if I would kindly condescend to do so, as the nearest farmhouse was not less than six miles away—an appalling distance to a tired and hungry man on a dark night. He did not think, he said, that I could ever reach it—even if I should be rash enough to try—in the Stygian darkness of a moonless night in the forest, more especially as I was a stranger in those parts; and that if I attempted to do so without a guide, I should most likely get lost in the forest for my pains. He apolo-

gized for the state of his miserable shanty and the
wretched accommodations he had to offer me, but
assured me that I was welcome to stay with the poor
nigger if I would consent to do so.   I told him that as
no choice in the matter seemed to be left me, I should
under the circumstances gladly avail myself of the
opportunity to remain with him.   Whereupon he
thanked me and bustled about the room making his
preparations for our frugal supper.   He set a pot of
coffee on some coals, and while this was boiling he
made two huge ashcakes, and put them in the fire.
Meat was scarce, he said, but he thought he might
have a few pieces still.   Searching about among some
greasy boxes and fire-blackened pie-pans, he found
one or two slices of old bacon, and some pieces of
salty meat-skins.   These were cooked on the coals;
and while they broiled and hissed and curled in fantastic shapes, he took his cakes from the ashes and
put them on a box that was to serve as a table.

At last all was done; and after serving me with
the best, keeping the meat-skins and the other refuse
for himself, he withdrew to a corner of the blazing
hearth, with his supper upon his knees, and fell to
with an appetite.   I am aware that many of my
readers will wonder how I could eat supper in such
a place, after the description I have given of it.   But
I was too hungry to be critical, or over-sensitive, and
I did eat it, and enjoyed it, too, perhaps with a zest
that many a dainty reader has never experienced.
The whitest bread never tasted sweeter than the
homely (and not over-clean) ashcake, and the rarest

of Mocha never gave forth a more delicious aroma than the black coffee-pot steaming upon the coals.

Our repast ended, the old negro cleared the things away, and brought out an old clay pipe and some home-grown tobacco, part of which he offered me. We sat down and conversed a while before the ruddy glow of the fire, until, a sense of weariness coming over me, I expressed a desire to retire to rest. My white-haired host had no better place to offer me than the pile of cottonseed. He pointed to it and sadly said that he "didn't hab no udder place but dat ar ter offer his mahster." I threw myself upon it, and for the first time in many months, fell almost instantly into a sound and peaceful slumber.

During the night, however, I was several times awakened by the sound of a voice, and as the fire was still burning, I could see the bowed form of the hoary old negro kneeling before the hearth in prayer. His cracked and trembling voice rang out in an earnest and pathetic petition to the Most High to save him from destruction. He knew, he said, that the sun of his life had nearly set. The plough was nearing the end of the furrow, and at any hour the feeble spark of his life might be forever extinguished. With tears of bitter sorrow streaming down his wrinkled cheeks, he begged in the name of Christ that his spirit might find an eternal resting-place among the great and the good who had gone before.

This earnest and melancholy prayer, repeated over and over again, and of which I have only given the bare substance, profoundly affected me, and I was

glad when he at length brought it to a close.
When I awoke next morning the first faint rays of
early daylight were stealing in through the openings
in the wall. My hard and uncomfortable bed of
cottonseed had given me sweeter and more refreshing
rest than a pillow of down could have done once, and
I experienced the buoyant feeling of renewed strength
and vigor. The old negro was seated on a rickety
chair before the blazing fire, and slices of bacon were
hissing on the coals, while a fresh supply of cakes
were roasting in the ashes. He greeted me with the
same air of old-fashioned politeness that had attracted
my notice the previous evening, and inquired if I had
rested well. He then placed my breakfast upon the
improvised table, and retired to a corner with his
own.

In half an hour I took leave of the good old darkey
and, having received some directions from him, I
went on my way. Later in the morning I found I
had missed my road the afternoon before, and I now
hastened to put myself right. The road which I then
pursued, and which I should have followed the previous day, was a leading thoroughfare, with a number of farm-houses at irregular intervals along its sides.
As I met on this highway a number of wagons, carts,
and other vehicles, I got a "lift" now and then from
some driver, and thus contrived to ride a good part
of the day.

It is needless to attempt to give, however, a detailed account of that day's journey. It was my
fourth morning out, and I had begun to lose all fear

of pursuit as I had thus far seen no evidence that any had been attempted. This thought was very encouraging as well as flattering, as it seemed to argue that I had covered up my tracks so well that pursuit had been rendered so difficult or impossible that very little had been attempted. This was precisely the case, though I did not know it at the time, nor until long afterwards.

I reached Marshall some hours after noon, but passed on through the city without stopping   Later in the day I got a "ride" or two from the obliging drivers of farm-wagons, and by this means traveled a much greater distance than would have been possible a-foot.   At sunset I came to a halt in front of a large house which had the appearance of being the abode of well-to do people.   Someone further back on the road had advised me to stop at this place—which was known as "Shaw Farm"—as being a suitable house at which to ask for accommodation for the night.   It was an extensive farm, and while its owner did not have the prestige that the possession of such a property, with its accompanying quota of slaves, would have given him under the old *régime*, he was well and favorably kown among his neighbor-people. His patrimonial estate was located, if I remember rightly, some five miles from the hamlet of Elysian Fields.

. A hallo at the gate brought a lady to the door, and with old-fashioned hospitality she invited me at once to "walk in," instead of impertinently demanding to know my "business" as the usual custom seems to be nowadays. I did not wait to be asked a second time, but entered at once and was shown into a well-appointed sitting-room where other members of the family were present. As soon as I was seated I told them that I was in search of a place at which to stop for the night, and that I had been advised to come to them. At the same time I warned them, as I never failed to do when soliciting a favor of this kind, that I had no money and could not remunerate them for their trouble. As to the extent of humiliation I was thus obliged to undergo almost every day, we shall leave the reader to judge. Mrs. Shaw replied to me very graciously and told me that I might remain if her husband were willing. Mr. Shaw, she said, was at the moment absent, on his way to the nearest postoffice. In about an hour he returned, bringing a large batch of mail and, when made acquainted with what had happened in his absence, he told me that I was welcome to such as they had, and that his family had done right in permitting me to remain. His wife appeared to be pleased at this compliment, and like the great-hearted lady she was, she bustled about "on hospitable thoughts intent."

With the harmless and not unkindly curiosity which we always find, perhaps more than anywhere else, among the farming classes of this section of the Union, Mr. Shaw asked me a great many questions. Among these were: "Where might you be going?" "Where are you from?" "What is your business?" "Are you a married man?" etc., etc. The last question always seems to possess great interest for the ladies present, and they wait for the answer with marked attention.   In the case of most of these inquiries, as well as of many similar ones, although I could not as a matter of course return answers as strictly truthful as I might have wished, I nevertheless replied readily and freely.   On all such occasions the poorest and least satisfactory direct response is looked upon with much more favor than the most elaborate evasion.   Indeed, at such times suitable answers are expected to the general class of questions outlined above.   Replies more or less evasive, or which are obviously equivocal, they regard as a just cause of suspicion, and the stranger is perhaps thereupon subjected to a fire of questions discharged at him from all sides, and which are not always remarkable for either delicacy or discrimination.

When supper was over we assembled in the sitting-room and passed an hour in social converse.   Then Mr. Shaw read aloud some extracts from late newspapers, and we were enabled to discuss the latest occurrences.   This was a new experience to me, as I had not for some years read any of the prominent daily or weekly journals, and thus was in profound ignorance of the leading news and events of the day. While I was thinking of this Mr. Shaw had taken up another newspaper and was glancing over it.   He now desired us to listen, and in the silence which ensued, he read aloud the following paragraph:

"Terrell, Texas: —Yesterday morning Mr. E. B. Fleming of Hopkins County, who has been an inmate of the asylum here for about three years, in some unknown manner made his escape. How he accomplished this is a profound mystery to all concerned. Search has been made for him in every direction, but without avail, as up to the present writing he has succeeded in eluding the vigilance of the officials. It would therefore appear that the chances for apprehending him are exceedingly precarious. His family, who reside in Sulphur Springs, were immediately notified."

"Well, well," said Mrs. Shaw, looking up with a scared face, "I wonder now if he will come through this way?"

"I guess not," laughed her husband. "But if he should, we could notify the sheriff and have him arrested. I don't believe," he continued, turning to me, "that lunatics ought to be allowed to wander at liberty over the earth in any such manner, and I think the asylum officers was very keerless in this here case. I hope they will git 'im back agin. What's asylums for, I'd like to know, if they're to let the lunatics git out, an' run about all over the face of creation?"

Then suddenly, and without the slightest warning, he looked over his glasses at me and asked me if I had ever been to Terrel. My heart, which was aleady beating painfully, flew into my mouth, and I glanced at him in alarm, to discern if possible his motive in putting such a question to me. Whether he had ulterior designs in asking such a question, I could not tell from his face; and hence I replied that I had.

"And did you," he pursued, "did you pay a visit to the asylum there?"

Controlling my agitation by a strong effort, I replied truthfully, that I had never "paid a *visit* to the asylum."

"Well, you ought," said he. And he thereupon launched out into a minute description of the asylum and its grounds, narrating many anecdotes of incidents which had occurred there. The conversation then took another turn, and I once more breathed freely.

When I retired to rest that night I did not enjoy the sound repose that fatigue usually induces. The feeling of confidence and security which had buoyed me up had received a severe shock; and I could not but realize that as the news of my escape had been telegraphed and published all over the State, some one might recognize me at any moment. I shuddered to think of the inevitable result of such a contingency. Even should any timid individual become suspicious of me, he had only to speak to the nearest country official, and my further progress would be arrested forever. It will perhaps be remembered that at this time I was wearing a suit of clothes of which every garment was indelibly branded with my full name and the name of the North Texas Insane Asylum, and so far I had not found any means by which these tell-tale marks could be effaced.

The inevitable corrollary from this was simply that in the future I must needs exercise the greatest apprehension. I could not fail to see that although the people whom I had met thus far on my journey had been almost uniformly kind and obliging, yet let them by any chance learn that I had for a term of years been an inmate of an insane asylum, and every man's hand would be turned against me. No-were, I am persuaded, do we find such superstitious horror of the insane as among the uneducated classes; and the unaffected kindness, courtesy, and ready hospitality now uniformly extended to me all along my route would be, if my history were known, changed in an instant to terror, harshness and per-secution. I knew that most if not all of the class mentioned possess the belief, once common among all people, whether high or low, that insanity is a blight sent down from heaven—an evil spirit, or devil, at work within us, or a curse of God. When people hold such a belief as this, I knew that I could expect no mercy from them, for it is a singular but indubitable fact that the kindest and most benevolent of men, where their affections are concerned can become, in matters appertaining to their religion, or their superstitious fears, stern, harsh, bigoted and intolerant.

These and other reflections drove sleep from my pillow for half the night; and before finally falling asleep I resolved to exercise greater care and vigilance always in my deportment towards those persons whom necessity compelled me to meet.

To the reader it may appear as somewhat singular that although I had stayed at quite a number of farm-houses since leaving the asylum, yet the names of none of the families are mentioned with the excep tion of Mr. Shaw's. The reason for this is simple. It was only at Shaw Farm that any incident out of the ordinary occurred to fix the name in my memory; while at each of the other country houses at which I stopped, no episode within my knowledge, nor circumstance of any kind, occurred to break the monotony of every-day events. Hence those names were no sooner heard than forgotten. But the name Shaw Farm and one other name, I believe, are the only ones which were impressed upon my mind at the time —the incident that has been detailed upon a former page having the effect of imprinting the name of the family indelibly upon my memory. This is why it has never been forgotten, while the other names did not stay in my recollection for a single day. This I regret, as it precludes the possibility of my ever being able to make just or adequate return —which of course was never demanded or expected, or even desired—to the good people who so generously, kindly and ungrudgingly gave me of their best. Without this whole-hearted hospitality on their part, —their prompt, willing and timely courtesy, my long journey had been ended before it had begun, and my hopeless eyes would still be gazing through the iron grates of my cell!

O generous friends, nameless but not forgotten, where shall I turn, in the cold and cruel world, to seek the unaffected kindness, the sincere hospitality, which ever marked your treatment of me? The culture, the polish, and the show of easy wealth are denied you; but higher than wealth, and purer than

the glitter and gloss of earthly pomp, your hearts
went out in sweetest sympathy toward mine; and
weary and heart-sore, gray with the dust of travel,
and bowed under the weight of years and sorrow,
you met me kindly—received me without question*
into the warmth and light of your firesides, and the
warmer glow of your hearts!

After midnight I sank into a restless and uneasy
slumber, broken by violent and disturbing dreams.
Visions of far-away dear ones came over my mind;
and I saw them sinking in treacherous quicksands,
falling down frightful precipices, or wandering in the
labyrinths of dark and trackless forests haunted by
savage Minotaurs. Finally I woke bathed in a
clammy perspiration, and saw that it was broad day.
Some one was knocking at my door and calling out
that breakfast was ready. I dressed myself hastily,
and joined the family in the dining-room. A feeling
of gloom and foreboding disaster oppressed me, and
I was glad to get away to be alone with my thoughts.
As I took leave of the family, Mrs. Shaw handed me
a savory-smelling package wrapped in a newspaper
and told me that it was "something for my lunch."

* In a journey of this kind, which cannot be pursued but for the
spontaneous kindness and generosity of the people, I question whether
the genuine and freehearted hospitality which extended to me
throughout, could be found by a ragged foot-traveler anywhere but
among the farmers of Texas. This acknowledgement, it seems to me,
is justly due to their brave, simple and generous spirit, and is made
without any desire to disparage or detract from the good qualities of
any other class, kind or condition of the people.

CHAPTER V.

All the world's a stage
And all the men and women merely players:
They have their exits and their entrances;
And one man in his time plays many parts.
—SHAKESPEARE.

The lunch furnished me by the kind-hearted Mrs. Shaw was ample, and supplied me with the first dinner I had had in many days. At noon I came upon a large spring which gushed from the bosom of the earth, and sent its pellucid stream down the moss-covered banks of a creek, in whose bed the waters came together and mingled. A huge shade-tree, whose leaves were tinted with the bright hues of the autumn, grew near at hand. At this spot I stopped, and furnished with water from the spring, enjoyed my lunch in comparative comfort. When this was done, an hour's repose among the gnarled roots of the oak restored my strength; and with renewed vigor and hope I rose and pursued my journey.

The air was crisp and cold to such a degree that I did not, as usual, suffer from heat; and I was thus enabled to travel a greater distance in a given time with less fatigue. Towards the close of day, on

102

making inquiries along the road, I was directed to the home of a family named Shaw as being somewhat better prepared than their immediate neighbors to give me accommodations for the night. A long and fertile lane led up to their gate, and as I turned into it I overtook a ragged and greasy negro; and he, mending his pace to agree with mine, walked along with me. I passed a few words with him, and as I neared the front of the house I was seeking, the negro, in pursuance of whatever business he was on, if any, turned aside and went off down a small by-lane which intersected the one I was in.

The lady of the house was in the yard as I came up, and when I had made known the nature of my errand, she looked at me sternly and suspiciously, and demanded:

"Are you not traveling with a negro?"

I hastened to reply, inwardly cursing the block-headed stupidity of the negro who had brought the suspicion of this hard-featured Amazon upon me:

"No, madam, I assure you I am not."

"Yet I saw you," she pursued, looking at me dis-trustfully, "I saw you come up the lane in company with one."

I opened my lips to speak. She interrupted me without ceremony.

"Do you pretend to say that I didn't?" she ex-claimed, raising her voice. "Do you mean to tell me to my very face—"

I interrupted her in my turn.

"Madam," said I, beginning to feel disgusted, "if

you do not intend to allow me to speak, say so, and I will go elsewhere; but if you are—"

Go on, she said.

"Well then," I resumed, "I cannot and do not deny that you saw me with the negro you complain of, but I overtook him, wholly by accident, at the end of the lane down there, and he walked along with me. That is all. I never saw him before. And besides, Mrs. Shaw, he claims to be a resident of your neighborhood."

This explanation appeared to satisfy her upon that score, yet did not wholly remove her distrust of me.

"You know my name, it seems," she replied. "How about that? Or did you guess it?"

"No, madam; I learned your name from one of your neighbors."

"And you want me to take you in for the night?" she next demanded.

I assured her that such was my desire.

"But I do not know you," she declared. "I never even heard of you. I never knew a man named Nall in my life. Besides," she asked, suddenly, and as if struck by a sudden thought, while she looked at me very straight, "how do I know but what you are an escaped lunatic?"

I glared at her in frightened silence for a moment.

"Do I look like one?" I said, desperately, restraining myself by a strong effort from turning about and making off at the top of my speed.

"No," she admitted, "you do not; but last spring a lunatic escaped from the Arkansas asylum, and came down here and put us to a world of trouble. He didn't look like a maniac, either."

A short silence ensued. I did not care to break it.

"But," she said, suddenly changing her tone after bending her head in thought for a moment, "while I cannot agree to take you in, as my husband is gone from home, and may not get back before late supper time, and there ain't nobody on the place but us women, you can come in and stay till my husband comes. I expect him in about an hour; and if he will let you stay, why it's all right with me."

I thanked her and followed her into the house.

The sun sank behind a wooded ridge in the west as we entered the door, and the air had grown cooler and damper. My conductress preceded me to the sitting-room, where she introduced me to an elderly lady who was knitting by the fire. We passed an hour in friendly chat,—or rather I should say small talk, as I am not so sure about its being very friendly. The good ladies seemed to have an idea that I might yet prove to be a swindler running away from some remote part of Texas; or a murderer; or a kind of monster belonging to the unclassifiables of Natural History; or perhaps they could not decide upon this point. But of one thing they were manifestly very sure; namely, that to whatever known or unknown part of the Animal kingdom I might belong, I nevertheless made it my business to roam about the earth and prey upon unprotected ladies—invading their homes, seizing them and destroying their lives, and forthwith roasting their quivering bodies in their best

Sunday "spiders," and then revelling in a cannibalistic feast.

Under such circumstances our conversation was not very friendly; for how could you exepçt two unprotected females, with a terrible Oger or Ghoul right before them to exercise their gentle tongues with their wonted irrepressible regularity? But if I go on at this rate the reader will doubtless conclude that my head is not so clear after all.

The ladies waited in some anxiety for Mr. Shaw; but he did not come until the clock was on the stroke of nine. He showed some surprise on seeing me but as soon as matters were explained to him, he told me with much cordiality that I might remain. We then sat down to a late supper.

The disturbing dreams that had haunted my slumbers the night before did not break in upon my repose that night. I slept sweetly and peacefully until the break of day.

On leaving this place after breakfast the following morning, I pursued my way in a southerly direction. The lines dividing the States of Louisiana and Texas were hardly three score miles away, and I expected to cross the Sabine near the close of the next day, or on the morning of the day following. For some reason, however, I missed my way, and got into a road which led me some distance away from the route it was my design to pursue. But unluckily, like most men who lose their bearings under similar circumstances, I neither knew at what point I had turned aside from the proper road, nor even discov-

ered that I had done so until it was too late to turn
back. Towards the middle of the afternoon, having
reached the environs of an unfamiliar "bottom,"
which grew out from the banks of a large creek, I so
bewildered myself in a maze or network of dim roads,
none of which seemed to lead anywhere except into
the trackless depths of the forest, that I very speedily
came to realize that I was lost. And not merely lost
as to the proper roads to follow, but lost as to
direction also. The realization or consciousness of
this fact which came home to me did not aid me any,
but on the contrary, tended to still further confuse
me.

The sky had been somewhat dark and threatening
from early dawn, and now the sun which might have
aided me by indicating which was south and which
north, became wholly obscured under leaden drifts
of clouds.

With the sky thus lowering in ominous-looking
banks above me, and myself hopelessly bewildered in
the unknown depths of the forest, my situation was
anything but pleasant.

Finally, in order that I might collect my thoughts
to decide upon some means of extricating myself
from so unpleasant a dilemma, I seated myself upon
a huge log which lay along the path I was pursuing.
On all sides, as far as the eye could see, the forest
extended—dark, silent and forbidding. The part in
which I then was—for the whole was seemingly interminable—was particularly wild and lonely. I
could see no evidence that human foot had ever

trodden those boundless solitudes before me. A deep silence seemed to brood over it, as if the very spirit of stillness itself had its abode there, save when the piercing call of the quail to its mate, or the sound of dropping nuts was heard. The underbrush grew in the wildest profusion beneath the great oaks or other monarchs of the forest.

A perfect picture of brooding loneliness and profound solitude greeted the eye wherever it was turned, even the semi-tropical verdure which waved in particolored masses on every hand having an indescribable air of useless magnificence and wasted grandeur.

Musing for a time upon these things, I was suddenly struck by the fact that even the scant daylight which remained was slowly but surely declining. Starting up upon this I resumed my journey, choosing only the roads which were more clearly defined and avoiding those that were dim and faint, in the hope that they might lead me sooner or later to some human habitation. The best of these roads were little more than bridle-paths, and whether they had been made by man, or by the horny hoofs of wandering quadrupeds was a question I should have liked much to solve. But the knowledge which might have saved me some hours of uneasiness or many miles of walking was wanting, and it only remained for me to trust to chance and patiently await the issue.

I had not gone a great distance when, in looking downward to pick my way around a dark lagoon covered with greenish-colored scum, I found a rusty

pocket-knife lying in my path. Elated by this discovery, which I felt to be indeed a fortuitous circumstance, I picked up the knife and examined it.
Originally a jack-knife of considerable size and
strength, some accident had reduced the number of
its blades from three to one, and deprived it of one
handle, while the whole knife was in such condition
as to render it almost useless for the purpose it was
originally intended for. Yet it was nevertheless a
welcome addition to my personal accoutrements.
After several failures, I contrived to open the remaining blade, and then scoured it thoroughly in the
moist sands under my feet. Thus after half an hour
of persistent labor I brightened the rusty steel to a
degree that hardly seemed possible at first.

It now remains for me to acquaint the reader with
my reasons for attaching so much importance to the
finding of the knife, if he has not already guessed
them. It will be remembered, no doubt, that mention
has been made more than once of the fact that each
of the garments I was wearing every day, and would
doubtless continue to wear for some time to come,
for want of means to obtain new ones, was branded
in indelible characters of considerable size, with my
own name in full, and the name of the North Texas
Insane Asylum; and that these names were so situated
as to be readily noticed by almost any one. It had
therefore taxed my ingenuity greatly since my escape
to so arrange my garments as to conceal these tell tale
characters; and while I had succeeded in doing this
to my entire satisfaction thus far, yet I knew that

an accident might at any time betray my secret so long as the letters remained.

Hence I was eager to take such steps as would forever prevent an occurrence so fatal to my hopes, and I knew of but one way to accomplish this; namely, to completely obliterate the damaging words with the blade of a sharp knife.

It will thus be seen why the finding of a cast-off jack-knife gave me such pleasure; and when I had put it in better condition for my purpose, it was with no little satisfaction that I entered upon the pleasant task of effacing the hateful words. This done I pressed forward· at a rapid and even pace, pursuing the wanderings of the path as it wound in and out among the trees of the forest in a manner which clearly indicated that no vehicle had ever passed over it. It led me over the broken and rotten trunks of trees, which lay prostrate across the path; around lagoons of stagnant water; past marshy swamps, covered with slime and ooze; over brush, sticks, stumps and stones. In this manner the remainder of the afternoon was spent, and I found myself no nearer the goal for which I had started. It was suffi-ciently evident that darkness would close down rapidly and soon, leaving me alone in the obscure labyrinths of a forest of which that portion at least was uninhabited save by prowling animals and mid-night owls. This thought spurred me on, but the shades of evening were falling rapidly around me, and the least indication of human presence remained yet to be discovered. Fortunately, however, the road

I was following was becoming brighter and broader, and this encouraged me to hope that possibly I might be able to keep to it even in the darkness. The shades of night were now falling fast, and the darkness was deepening with a speed which seemed to me to be almost fatal. Yet I did not despair, but determined to walk the whole night through, if I could keep to the road, rather than stop anywhere in the lonely precincts of the wood. The darkness, when it came at last, was profound, as such nights always are in the forest. There was no moon, or at least none was visible through the dark banks of cloud, but I pushed on, as I could yet see the vague and dim outlines of the road. My pace was necessarily much slower, and I began to feel the fatigue of the day's journey. Now and then in my haste I ran into shallow lagoons of stagnant, and often ill-smelling water, or into obstructions less unpleasant but more painful. The moments went by, but slowly, and the solemn hush of night settled over the forest. The hooting of many owls, which echoed through the wood, sounded weird and unearthly in the silence, and whatever superstitious fears I might have had— and we all possess them—came back to me now. Other sounds, not so wild or supernatural, but of far deeper import, as coming from animals known to be desperate or dangerous, came to my ears from the distance, faint and soon dying away. Winged creatures whirred past me in the darkness, and innumerable insects buzzed and chirped in the air.

Finally I thought I caught the distant flicker of a

light; but ere I could assure myself of the fact, it
vanished as suddenly as it came. I then retraced my
steps to what I conceived to be the point at which I
had first seen it, and looked searchingly in that direction, yet nothing but darkness met my eye. Deciding that an optical delusion of some kind, which often
occurs to men under similar circumstances, had
probably deceived me, I gave over the vain attempt
to find a light that very likely did not exist, and pursued my journey. But after walking a short distance,
the light flashed out upon my sight again; and this
time in a manner which led me to conclude that it
was no optical delusion after all, but a real light.
As it appeared to be at no great distance from where
I stood, and was gleaming with a steady and even
glow directly in the path I was pursuing I held on my
way without stopping. As I approached, I could
clearly perceive that the light shone from an uncurtained window, and it came from a glass lamp which
burned with a steady flame upon what I took to be a
table. With much satisfaction at the discovery—
which promised shelter, rest and good cheer—I hurried forward, and soon stood before the dark outlines
of a comfortable looking cottage.

Not wishing to enter the yard until I was assured
that no fierce watch-dog would attack me, I called
out the usual formula at the gate. It was necessary,
however, to repeat my halloo before anyone heard
me; and then, after a short silence, followed by the
sound of footsteps and the opening of the door, a
deep voice called out to know "who was there?"

To which I replied, "A stranger."

A dissatisfied "Humph" followed this admission, and the voice demanded:

"And what is a stranger doing here at this hour of the night, and what does he want?"

My interlocutor appeared to be standing upon a sort of piazza in front of the house, and to regard all strangers as objects of suspicion.

I replied that I was an entire stranger in that part of the State, was lost, foot-sore and weary, and in search of a place at which to pass the night.

A silence of considerable duration followed; then the voice demanded:

"Who are you, sir, and where are you from?"

I own that I felt somewhat irritated at his cold and inhospitable reception—this stern and suspicious treatment from a man who was bound, as soon as I made known my distress, to receive me courteously.

"My name, sir," I returned, sternly and curtly, "is Nall. I started with my wagons from Blank, and got lost from them. I attempted to take a shorter road a-foot, and missed my way."

"Where are you going?" he next inquired.

"From Eagletopper to Browntown."

"From Eagletopper* to Browntown!" exclaimed the voice, sharply and suspiciously. "And what are you doing in this out-of-the-way part of —— Bottom, if you are really trying to get to Browntown? The road which leads to that place is twenty miles back."

* These names are fictitious. For reasons entirely personal the true names are withheld,

Then in a sharper, louder tone, full of distrust and suspicion, the man turned about, as if with the intention of immediately entering the house, and added:

"Mr. Stranger, you must give a better account of yourself if you would have me think you an honest man. I don't like your tale!"

I hastened to say that "I had got myself completely lost, and could find no one to set me right, and I had naturally followed the road which appeared to be traveled the most; that I was utterly worn out and exhausted, and among strangers, and could only throw myself upon his mercy."

This appeal had its effect; for though the man did not reply, he came on down the steps and opened the gate. I entered, and he said, speaking in a manner somewhat more civil, "that though he had no accomodations for strangers, he would take me in, and give me the best they had, such as it was."

Upon this, I stopped him for a moment and said:

"I feel it is but fair that I should tell you, here and now, that I have no money to offer you in return for your hospitality, and therefore cannot pay you anything."

"Well," he replied, as we mounted the steps, "that need make no difference. As you have had the honesty to tell me so in advance, I will be as plain with you. You are welcome, sir, to our poor accommodations, and I hope you will not think anything of my manner of receiving you just now. No offense was intended, but the hour was late for us, and this is

a part of the world where strangers seldom come."
I could not help thinking that if this were true,
it was all the more reason for treating the few who
did come with greater courtesy. But, although the
excuse he gave was quite as remarkable as my reception had been, I merely thanked him, and we entered
the house together.

He conducted me into the room where I had first
seen the light, and introduced me to his wife—a white-
haired old lady sitting before the fire. She was the
only occupant of the room, and I learned that she and
my host lived entirely alone. As to the latter, no
sooner had he and I reached the light, than, as if by
a mutual impulse, we turned and gazed upon each
other with some curiosity. Notwithstanding his vigorous step and strong voice, I was surprised to find
my host to be a man apparently not far from three
score and ten. His hair was white and wavy, and
a long beard depended from his chin; but his eyes
were clear, resolute and undimmed by age. His
long full upper lip was closely shaven, and his
mouth set in a firm straight line. Though his
shoulders were slightly rounded, he yet held himself
with an erectness many a younger man might have
envied. His eyes were blue and kindly, and his whole
countenance was that of a man honest and firm in
his principles, of a nature deeply religious, kind and
obliging to his neighbors, but rigid in his ideas of
duty and moral behavior, merciless to the wrong-doer,
terrible in anger when aroused, and in spirit, bold,
daring and dauntless.

This good opinion that I had formed of him increased as I came to know him better; and uninvit-
ing as my reception had been, the night spent with
the solitary old couple was much pleasanter than I
could have anticipated. Their courtesy was blunt,
but kindly, and I did not need to be told that it came
from their hearts. The old house-wife bustled about
and set before me a tempting repast, to which I was
disposed to do ample justice; and the steaming cup
of coffee she placed upon my right spread its genial
warmth over my tired frame. It was pleasant to a
wanderer to emerge from the dark, forbidding and
owl-haunted forest into the light and warmth of a
happy fireside; and a restful feeling of pleased content stole over me as we sat before the blazing hearth.
The evening of life, however dark its shadows might
have been, had not chilled the hearts nor dimmed
the minds of this white-haired couple. They presented a perfect picture of hale and hearty old age,
whose hearts were unsullied by the memory of
a single unworthy act. The ruddy glow of the fire-
light played over their sober countenances as they
related to me many incidents of their past; and as
they talked, each suggesting some episode that the
other had forgotten, I could not but feel that every
human life, no matter how lowly and obscure, has
always its romantic side. However unknown or
unsuspected it may be, there is yet, in almost every
breast, consecrated but not dimmed by the flight of
time, the details of some early romance whose mere
memory will thrill and stir the heart.

It was growing somewhat late when we rose from our places at the fireside and retired to rest; and the fatigue of the day's exhausting though fruitless journey overcoming me as I laid my head upon the pillow, I sank at once into a profound and restful slumber.

They roused me in time for an early breakfast, and this meal being over, I and my new-found friends —for as such I could not help regarding them—parted with mutual and sincere expressions of amity and good will. Having received the necessary instructions from my aged host, as to how to set myself straight I set forth upon my journey.

It is a source of much disappointment to me that I cannot recall the names of this good old couple. For in this place if in no other I should like to make some return for their warm and grateful hospitality. But of all the names of the many who gave me the freedom of their homes, without hope of reward, I can only, as has been stated, recall the names of but two or three. This is greatly to be regretted, but cannot be remedied; and when I parted from those kind friends at the time, we paretd, in all probability, forevermore.

I crossed the Sabine River on the following day, and breathed freer when I found myself upon the soil of Louisiana. As long as I remained in Texas the danger of pursuit and capture was real, and necessitated a long course of downright deception on my part which became more repugnant every day. And had I been captured, the falsehoods which I had been obliged to tell would not, had they been found out (and a falsehood, like a boomerang, generally returns to him who sends it) have turned the scale in my favor.

The direction I took was south, and I pursued my way through a dense wooded district. Indeed the forest extended in several directions for more miles than one would have cared to walk, if, like myself, he had already traveled for several hundred miles a-foot. The first night I passed in this State was spent at a farmhouse near the roadside; the second —but let us not anticipate. Yet I may say that I can never recall the occurrences of that second night in Louisiana without a sensation very near akin to horror.

On the afternoon of this second day, having wandered away from the public thoroughfare—which was itself quite dim at times—in consequence of some ambiguous directions given me by a block-headed farmer, I came to a part of the country which was pretty lonely, and from its appearance bade fair to become still more so. While ruminating upon the probable outcome of this new misfortune as well as the best course to be pursued in such an exigency, I met two peasant women coming a-foot along the road, and stopped to ask them some questions as to route, etc. As the information they gave me did not agree with my pre-conceived ideas of the route I designed to pursue, I hesitated somewhat before making up my mind to act upon it. Among those who have ever traveled to any extent on foot or by

private conveyance through the country, it is notorious that directions about roads given by ladies are as
often as not—so far as any practical benefit is concerned—a very Sphinx's Riddle. On this occasion,
however, as I had no better authority to appeal to,
I received their rambling descriptions of the topog-
raphy of the country with deference; thanked them,
and proceeded on my way.

One of the women had with her a small yellow dog
—called by the vulgar a "bench-leg fice"—but as
there was nothing about it particularly inviting or
attractive, I scarce gave it a passing glance. It may
be that this was looked upon as an intentional "slight"
by the dog, and resented as such; or on the other
hand it may be that doggy did not like my appearance. However that may have been, I had gone but
a few steps when I heard the swift patter of light feet
behind me, and almost at the same instant I felt a
sudden, sharp, and stinging pain in my foot just
above the heel, and whirling suddenly, was just in
time to see a small yellow object flying down the
sandy road towards the two women at the top of its
speed, and howling at every leap. Then I knew that
the small dog had sneaked up behind me and bitten
me upon those cords and sinews of the foot most
used in walking.

For a moment I was so angry that I could hardly
restrain myself; while, to add to my mortification
and discomfiture, the two females broke out into a
loud shout of laughter. They seemed to enjoy the
situation very much, and the echoes of their cach-

innation could have been heard, I am sure, almost a
quarter of a mile.   This was the "last straw;" and
too enraged to keep silent, I told them that if I had
the dog within my reach, I would kill him. This barbarous proposal shocked them so much, that, calling
out encouragingly to their dog, which had probably
scented danger in the air, and had struck out in a
wild run towards home, its fright increasing with every
leap towards safety until it had gone nearly insane
through fear,—they turned upon me, heaping upon
me every opprobrious epithet, every scurrilous accu-
sation, every vulgar denunciation which their narrow
vocabulary could command.

    I did not, however, remain to witness this explo-
sion of vulgar and splenetic rage; but turned and
walked away, leaving the angry females to follow
the footsteps of their cherished dog.   The wound in
my foot pained me considerably, but I did not stop.
The sun had passed the meridian some hours before,
and was slowly sinking.   The road I was pursuing
—if road it could be called—was vague and dim, and
there did not appear to be a human dwelling along
its entire length.   At all events I did not pass any,
nor meet a single individual from whom directions
could be had.   Hoping, however, that a farm-house
might come in sight any moment, I pressed on instead of turning back.   In this manner the afternoon
waned, and the misery in my foot had degenerated
to a dull, throbbing ache with a keen dart of pain
now and then as I lifted my foot incautiously.   The
road had become dimmer, and the appearance of the
country more wild and lonely.

As sunset approached I entered the outskirts of a forest, and from changes in its aspect, I became aware in about an hour that a considerable stream was near at hand. A few minutes later it was a forest no longer, but a wilderness. Rank vegetation and matted undergrowth were seen on every hand, and small streams meandered in all directions. My road led me finally down into the bed of a considerable creek. The bottom was covered with pebbles and sand, and though the stream was wide, the water was clear and shallow. The bank on the opposite side was sloping, forming a gentle declivity which led from the surface of the earth down to the water below, and I inferred that at this particular spot the stream was usually forded, as above and below the banks were precipitous, and the current deep and swift. After a moment's deliberation I removed my shoes, rolled my trousers up to my knees, and waded across to the other side. The water was cold, but hardly so deep as I had anticipated. On emerging from the water I sat down upon a boulder and replaced my foot-gear. Upon toiling up the sandy bank I found that I had probably committed an error, as no road could be found. It seemed to end abruptly in the pebbly bed of the creek. Hoping, however, to find some trace of it, or perhaps another one somewhere in the vicinity, I hastily searched the woods before me for more than a mile. But all in vain. Not the faintest sign of a road or even a bridle-path could be found. I turned, therefore, to retrace my steps to the ford, which I supposed to be about a mile away, when suddenly and without the least warning my injured foot gave out, and I sank down upon the ground, unable to advance another step. For a moment I closed my eyes in sheer despair—but only for a moment. Raising myself then to a sitting posture, and looking about me, I saw with something akin to alarm that I had fallen in a veritable wilderness. A jungle stretched away on either hand, the rank undergrowth forming such thickets that no eye could see through them. Small openings, or glades, appeared now and then in the more open parts of the forest, and some yards from where I lay a small stream, partially hidden by an intervening mass of tangled vines and fallen tree-tops, ran brawling along; while only a few feet away, upon my right, a small quantity of water had collected in a sort of minute basin, or sink in the earth.

The sun was setting. His last rays, grown redder now, fell over the dreary prospect, touching everything with golden fire. The dependent vines and matted undergrowth were motionless and still. No air was stirring. A wilder or more lonely spot I had never seen, and a silence that was absolute and oppressive brooded over all. Too wild a spot altogether, I reasoned, for any man, crippled and unarmed, to remain in, and I resolved to make an effort to get back to the ford.

I then examined my wounded foot. Removing the shoe, which had become so tight as to be painful, I found that the ankle and the parts immediately around it were swollen and discolored. The injured

member had not filled up the shoe sooner on account
of its being much too large for me.   The flesh was
burning hot and throbbing painfully.   With my shoe
in my hand I crawled toward the handful of water a
few feet away.   The anguish occasioned by the
moving of my wounded foot was exquisite, and almost
more than I could bear.   I progressed but slowly,
moving an inch at a time.   Reaching the water finally,
I found it to be clear and cold, and the grateful cool-
ing sensation imparted to my swollen foot by bathing
it in the precious liquid granted me a temporary
respite from suffering.   I bathed it thoroughly; but
when this was done I did not have the fortitude to
undergo the acute torture which would inevitably
accompany an attempt to return to the spot where I
had fallen; and in any case there was no good reason
for it that I could see; so I lay down my the water
and elevated my injured leg my means of a convenient rise in the ground.

The pain abating, an overpowering sense of fatigue
stole over me; I heard the pleasant noise of falling
water as one whose senses were enthralled; and then
all became blank.

The noise of some animal aroused me.   I lay still
and listened, and could distinctly hear the footfalls
of some heavy quadruped crunching on the dead
leaves.   The sounds appeared to come from the opposite side of the stream; and as the moon was now
shining, though not very brightly, I raised my head
softly and peered over the tops of the intervening
undergrowth.   What I saw filled me with alarm, but

I did not withdraw my head in the fear of making a
noise. On the high ground upon the opposite side of
the stream a large bear, followed by two cubs, was
approaching at a steady pace. She came on down
the bank of the creek to the edge of the water, where
she paused, sniffed the air, and went to lapping the
water. The distance which separated us was about
twenty yards, as near as I could judge, and I mar-
velled that the wonderful instinct common to every
member of the animal kingdom, did not warn her of
the proximity of a foe. Indeed, I had not the
smallest doubt that it would do so and I resolved
upon the instant that if the shaggy monster attacked
me, I would feign death, as I had read somewhere that
bears will not molest a corpse. But this, happily,
was not necessary, as the bear did not offer to attack
me, nor even appear to be aware of my presence.
She drank her fill of water in what I took to be a
very leisurely and deliberate manner, and then, turning awkwardly, shuffled on up the bank in the way
she had come, and disappeared in the forest.

Waiting some miuntes in order to be sure that she
did not return, I hurriedly replaced my shoe, which
I could now do without inconvenience, I rose to my
feet and found that the act of walking did not occasion me greater pain than I could bear. I then limped
cautiously but rapidly away in a contrary direction
to that which the bear had pursued. The moon
rode high in the heavens, shedding a dim uncertain
light over the forest. I supposed that the night was
more than half gone, and my repose had greatly refreshed me.

Without road, path, or beaten way to guide me, I
struck out into the shadowed depths of the forest,
choosing my course as best I could over the moss-
grown trunks of trees, piles of rotten brush-wood,
past swinging vines that hung in my path, and under
the green arches of umbriferous trees. Coming after
a time to a good-sized creek or bayou, I determined
to choose my course along its banks, hoping that it
might ultimately lead me to some inhabited place.
Accordingly, I went on down its serpentine banks,
limping painfully, as my wounded foot still hurt me,
but making very fair progress.

I had not gone far in this manner when in passing
beneath the widespreading boughs of a huge old tree
I found that the ground was covered with a large
number of immense acorns known in vulgar parlance
as the *overcup acorn*. I stopped to gather some,
when, hearing a sudden movement in the branches
above me, I instinctively paused. The next moment
a dreadful scream rang out from some part of the
tree above me with bood-curdling intensity. It was
a terribe prolonged wailing scream that echoed far
and wide through the forest, and which struck the
silence and stillness of terror to my heart. I knew
the sound. I knew that that fearful scream could
come from no other throat but that of a panther.
The next moment I heard the fierce animal move,
and in the terror and fright of the moment I turned
and fled at the top of my speed from the vicinity of
the accursed tree. If anything were wanting to complete my terror, it came in less than a minute.

Another fierce scream rose on the air as I ran, and added to my speed. I fled through the forest as fast as my legs would carry me, leaping obstructions that I could never have leaped in calmer moments, and contriving to avoid numerous limbs and thorny vines that blocked my way. In this manner I ran for nearly a mile, taking no thought of direction or distance, but conscious only of a desire to get as far as possible from the panther. Finally I stopped to recover my breath, which was so far spent that I could run no further, and remembering my wounded foot suddenly, which I had completely forgotten in my fright, I found that I could now walk upon it without pain. This astonished me greatly, and I paused to examine the injured flesh more closely, as I could not understand the sudden transition from a state of pain and soreness to a condition in which, whether it was well or not, it no longer pained me.

I found that there was still a sensation of screness about the ankle, but I could walk upon it without limping. Rejoicing, therefore, at the sudden restoration of the wounded member, I rested a few minutes on a fallen log and proceeded on my way.

In my fright I had run away from the stream I had been following, and I did not attempt to find it again. As earlier in the night I traveled on through the trackless forest with neither path nor road to guide me. At this point the moon, never bright, went behind a cloud low down in the sky, and I found myself in total darkness. I paused in dismay, and knew not which way to turn. But as my eyes became

more accustomed to the darkness I determined to push
on my way not deeming it advisable to stop. I went
along slowly and carefully, feeling along, as it were,
so as to avoid the chance of running into any obstruction.

But presently, in putting out my foot to take a
cautious step, I felt it descend upon space, the earth
gave way beneath my other foot, and I felt myself
slipping down a steep declivity. I endeavored to
stay my progress by grasping at tufts of grass and
other vegetation which grew out from the bank (for
such it was) but vainly, and I slipped on down. Then
without warning I felt my feet entering some ice-cold
fluid, and in another moment was up to my chin in
the chilling current of a stream. Gasping for breath,
and chilled to the bone, I made several abortive
attempts to scramble out. But the next instant,
clutching by accident the trunk of a small sapling
growing near the water, I renewed the attempt with
better success and got out upon the bank.

I then observed that instead of going behind a
cloud, as I had supposed, the moon had sunk, and
day was fast breaking. My plight was a sad one.
My clothes, dripping with the ice-cold waters of the
creek, clung to my flesh with all the tenacity of
water-soaked garments and added to my discomfort.
My teeth were chattering with cold, and I realized
that vigorous muscular exercise was my best resource
under the circumstances. For more than an hour I
walked rapidly back and forth under the trees, swinging my arms as I went, and contriving to keep

warmer than one might have thought possible.

By this time the sun had risen, and was peeping over the distant tree-tops. His genial rays were warming the world into life, and I turned about and went rapidly towards the east. In less than two hours I came to a ford on another large bayou and, on the dry warm sands which stretched between the water and the banks, I removed my wet clothes. I wrung them out carefully, and laid them upon the sands to dry. While the sun was accomplishing this, aided by the breeze, I resumed my exercise; and looking about me carefully I saw a plain well-defined road leading out from the bed of the bayou and disappearing over the banks above. This welcome discovery renewed my courage and the hope that perhaps I might make my way that morning out of the desolate wilderness, and find some farmhouse or cabin where I might get rest and food, of which latter I stood greatly in need.

In something less than an hour the sun, assisted in no small degree by a warm breeze which blew from the south had dried my clothes sufficiently for me to wear them without a great deal of discomfort. I thereupon dressed myself in my scanty suit, and proceeding to the road which I had observed, followed it up to the firmer ground above me. Here, directing my anxious gaze to the various points of the compass I was delighted to see a small unpainted farmhouse standing in a secluded part of the forest. So far as I could observe it was completely isolated. The distance I judged to be not greater than a quarter of

a mile from where I stood. Overjoyed at the prospect of rest and shelter, for I was very greatly worn
and exhausted—so much so indeed that I felt I should
have perished in the wilderness or been devoured by
wild animals in another day—I hurried on towards
the farmhouse—for such I judged it to be.

When I reached the yard gate a few minutes later,
I first satisfied myself that there were no fierce watch-
dogs to seize me, and I then entered and knocked at
the door. Presently it opened, and I was surprised
to find an old negro. standing before me. I knew
from the mean appearance of the house, and its
neglected and poverty-stricken appearance that its
occupants were too poor to keep servants; hence I
rightly judged, when the negro appeared in answer
to my knock, that he was the master of the house.
He greeted me with the old-fashioned courtesy of
the *aute-bellum* slave, and I made known my wants
to him. He replied that I was welcome to all he
had, and that I might enter. He then led the way
into an apartment—not over clean—used as a sitting-
room where his wife, a fat old negress with a dingy
handkerchief bound about her woolly head, sat smoking a dirt-begrimed pipe in one corner of a commodious fireplace. I went immediately forward and
warmed my chill frame in the homelike glow of the
fire.

"Mahse Nall," said the motherly old negress, a
typical "black mammy" of the old *regeme*, as I turned
my steaming form before the cheerful blaze, "hab
youse had enny breckfuss dis mawnin'?"

I told her that I had not, nor any supper, either, the previous evening, and was nearly famished. Knocking the ashes from her black clay pipe, she laid it on the mantel-piece and went into the kitchen.

The kind old negro, who remained in the room, could not do enough for me, and hovered about offering his services in a hundred ways, *and never for a moment allowed me to forget the social chasm between us.*

By the time my clothes were thoroughly dried, the old negress set some breakfast before me, and what a breakfast it was to my famished eyes! Delicious ham, fresh-laid eggs, golden butter, and the whitest bread, all laid on a snowy table cloth. A pot of steaming coffee, with cream and sugar, completed the details of the repast, and meal was never enjoyed more heartily. My evident enjoyment of their good cheer obviously gave great pleasure to the kind old couple. They watched me closely, and as I proceeded they nodded and winked at each other and made other signs denoting the highest gratification— keeping up a constant pantomimic communication between themselves comically expressive of the child-like satisfaction they felt in being able to give me so much pleasure. When I had finished, the old negress, with a laugh of gratified vanity, asked me whether I had enjoyed my breakfast, and she waited, with a comic grin of self-complacency, as though she didn't know just what my answer would be. I praised it so highly that she swelled with pompous self-importance, while her squat black figure bustled about in

various little attentions to the man who had shown
so high an appreciation of her *cuisine*.

I went back with them into their sitting-room and
sat for a while before the fire. While thus comfort-
ably toasting myself, the old negro expressed his wonder that I had come out of the forest alive.

"Dem ar painters," he said, "is allers dar. Dey's
all ober dem ar woods, an' de swamps is fuller b'ars.
We uns here kin hear de painters a-screamin', an' I
tells yer, Mahse Nall, whin I'se in dem ar woods, an'
hears a painter, dis yere nigger am *a-gwine* fum dat
place, an' he aint er gwiner be long 'bout it. No,
sir. An' he aint gwine back no mo, I doan want no
truck widdum. Dey lubs nigger meat too well." He
paused a moment and resumed:

"We's got a boy here—de unly chillun we's got.
He's mos grown now, an' he thinks he's biggern we
is. He went out in dem woods, two or free miles
fum here, wid my gun. Roamin' roun' out dar," he
continued, in a tone of lofty contempt, "in sum
woods he didn' know nuffin' about, an' den he had
ter go an' git loss. An' de fust thing he knowed a
big painter got after him. Den he lit out an' run.
An,' Mahes Nall," he went on in a tearful voice, "he
was skeered so bad dat he drapped de gun—he frowed
my gun away."

And the memory of his loss—the gun thus reck-
lessly thrown away—affected him so much that the
tears started to his eyes.

"Dat boy," he resumed, after a melancholy pause,
"he cum a flyin' home, sked nylly ter deff—his eyes

big as dem sassers, an' he couldn' disricerlick whut he
done wid de gun. Nebber in dis world," he continued, pathetically, "whar he put dat gun.   An' de
nex day I say say I: 'Lookee here, nigger, youse
my chillun, but you fool, das whut you is. You ain't
got no sense, an' you fine my gun. You go hunt my
gun, an' you brung hit back here.   Ef yer doant,
youse 'ud better—

"An' he went, Mahse Nall," he concluded, in the
tone of one about to burst into tears, "an' nebber
cum back no mo'.   We's nebber seed 'im sense."

The recollection of this double misfortune stirred
them deeply, and the old negress broke out into a
loud fit of weeping.   For some moments they wept
and moaned in a most disconsolate and heart-broken
manner. I endeavored to console them, and presently
succeeded to a surprising degree.   With the change-
able and impulsive feelings of their race, they passed
quickly and easily from one extreme to another, and
were soon laughing in the most light-hearted manner
imaginable.

I then entertained them for an hour with some of
the marvelous stories that every negro so loves to
hear; and finally, feeling greatly the need of repose,
I told them I would like to lie down in some quiet
place and sleep for a few hours. My black host thereupon conducted me to a small building in one corner
of the yard, apparently used as a granary, and told
me I might rest there as long as I pleased.   I requested him to wake me about the middle of the
afternoon, in case I should still be sleeping at that

hour, in order that I might depart upon my journey. He promised this and withdrew. I threw my tired frame upon a soft pile of "seed-cotton," probably now for the first time used for such a purpose, and in a few minutes was sound asleep.

When I woke the kind hearted old negro was standing beside my improvised couch, regarding me with an expression of simple and childlike benevolence. I started up and inquired the time of day. My question, however, was answered before he spoke. I could see through an uncurtained window that it was near sunset.

"Thunder!" I exclaimed, "I have overslept myself."

"Hit's sundown," said the negro. "I cum in here ter woke yer up *awhilergo*, but you wus a-sleepin' so soun' dat I couldn' woke yer yit."

"Well," I rejoined, "it is all right. I haven't quite finished my nap yet, anyway, and so will not get up. You need not trouble about rousing me again, until I wake of my own accord."

I then lay back upon the soft pile of cotton and in an instant was unconscious. When I came to myself the second time the sun was shining broadly in upon me, and for a minute I could not remember where I was. But supposing from the situation of the sun that it wanted but a few hours of night, I started up hastily. My long sleep had dazed me somewhat and, I felt a little unsteady upon my feet.

A single glance around, as I became more fully awake, reminded me of my location. Walking towards the door, which had been left ajar, I had started towards the gate when a familiar voice called after me. I turned and saw my old black host standing on the steps of the farmhouse. After a moment's hesitation I turned and started towards him, a little perplexed in my own mind as to whether I ought to resume my journey at once, or stop for another hour or two. But my host had already decided the question for me.

"Yo' breckfuss am reddy," he said, as I approached.

"Breakfast!" I exclaimed. "Supper you mean."

He grinned knowingly.

"No, sah!" he ejaculated, emphatically. "Hit's mawnin', an' breckfuss am reddy."

I looked up at the sun. To me it appeared to be within a few hours of setting in the west, and I said so. My host laughed gleefully in the consciousness of superior knowledge.

"Youse turned roun'," he said. "Dat's whut you is. Youse turned roun'. Dat's de wes'," he continued, with a comical assumption of profound erudition, as he pointed directly away from the sun.

"Dat's de wes', an' dat's de eas'. Youse turned roun' Mahse Nall, das whut *you* is. An' you tho't," he continued, just as though such a thing had never been heard of before, "*dat* wus de wes'. But, naw, sah, hit aint. Dat's de wes'," pointing again, and keeping his arm leveled for a long while. "Yas sah. Das hit."

The simple old negro was greatly elated in having so far triumphed over me as to be able to instruct me regarding the art of finding the different points of the compass, and was eager to have his wife share his triumph with him.

We then entered the house, and in a few moments another delightful breakfast was set before me, the negroes taking seats near at hand where they could watch and enjoy the evident pleasure I found in doing the fullest justice to such admirable cooking. I again expressed my approval in the broadest and most flattering terms, and again my hostess found in herself an object of gleeful self-congratulation. Indeed though I felt sure that I enjoyed the well-cooked repast as only a hungry man could, yet the pleasure they experienced in seeing my enjoyment seemed greater than my own.

When breakfast was over I expressed my purpose of immediately departing upon my journey. They urged me strongly—nay, *begged* me to remain at least another day, and I was much inclined to do so, but I realized that I ought—and indeed *must*—set forth upon my journey. Finding their entreaties were of no avail, they ceased to importune me, and the benevolent old negress told me to wait a few minutes and she would prepare a nice lunch for me. This I very willingly did, as I always preferred to have some food with me, so that in any emergency I should not have to go hungry.

Presently she came back, the floor quivering and shaking beneath her solid tread, bringing a great paper full of good things—enough to last two hungry men a whole day. I did not like to receive so much, and protested that half as much would do me, for I knew they were poor and had none too much, but they pressed it upon me, refusing to reduce the size of the package by so much as a single biscuit, and I accepted it as it was offered.

They then entreated me to find their boy—with whose name and description they furnished me—if I could, somewhere in my travels, and let him understand that he need not, even if he had thrown away their gun, feel obliged to conceal the secret of his whereabouts from them; and that they earnestly entreated him to return. I assured them that they might rely upon me to find him if it were possible, and urge him to return; and this promise manifestly gave them great pleasure.

Having received explicit instructions as to how to proceed, without again losing myself in the forest, I set out on my way with a lighter heart, and with renewed energy. The prospect of presently getting out of an almost interminable forest, in whose dark depths I had gone astray, without again involving myself in a like predicament was so encouraging that I traveled all morning at a brisker pace. The road I pursued led me for another day through a lonely and dreary forest which stretched away for a number of miles on either hand; but the roadway itself was so plain and easily followed that I did not become bewildered in the many paths and small roads which intersected it. During that day I passed, too, an isolated farmhouse at irregular intervals, and thus was spared the desolate feeling of utter loneliness which always oppressed me when traveling through an uninhabited section of country.

CHAPTER VI.

Ah! there are moments for us here when seeing
Life's inequalities and woes and care,
The burdens laid upon our mortal being
Seem greater than the human heart can bear.

PHOEBE CARY,

On the Atchafalya Bayou, which forms the outlet
of Red River, and is the connecting link between
that stream and the Father of Waters, there is a bay
of considerable extent formed by the abrupt widen-
ing and subsequent narrowing of the Atchafalya. It
is known in that section as Berwick's Bay; but
whether it is called by that name on the maps—or,
indeed, is on the maps at all—the present writer
does not know. A small town is situated on the bay,
called Morgan City; though it is also, and perhaps
more generally, known as Berwick's Bay; and this
name is applied to either the village or the bay, or
both.

It was towards this place that I now made my
way, traveling, in the manner already described, over
the extensive prairie lands in that region, which bear
no small resemblance to many parts of Texas, and
which reach for a great number of miles in every
direction. Since my late experiences in the wilder-

137

ness, I had determined to avoid such places in the future, as far as possible; for I had no desire to re-peat in the dark depths of some unknown forest, the adventures of that night in the jungle.

One afternoon I learned by inquiry along the road that a wild and untraveled forest, which doubtless gave retreat to many dangerous quadrupeds, was not far ahead of me, and that I should probably have some difficulty in getting through its mazes safely. More-over, this forest was no less than fifteen miles in width, and was, therefore, more extensive than any I had yet passed through. When this information was communicated to me, by a horseman whom I met in the road, the afternoon was so far spent that sunset was only an hour away. I therefore imme-diately determined that I would go no further than the nearest farmhouse, if I could induce its inmates to give me lodging, and I inquired of my good-natured informant as to the probable number of houses I should pass between that hour and sunset.

He replied: "Only one."

"Is this country, then," I asked "a desert—an uninhabited waste?"

"Well, no," he answered, smiling; "not that, exactly; but in this region hereabouts settlements are few and far between. The house I speak of you will find about a mile or so away, right on down this road. It belongs to a rich planter named Johnson. You will not have to go far out of your way to get there, as this road will take you past the gate."

I thanked him, and he added as he rode away:

"You had best be careful as to how you let Johnson
turn you away, unless you want to make your bed
with the wolves."

From this friendly warning I gathered that the
wealthy planter had an unpleasant habit of shutting
his door in the face of such humble travelers as
myself, and the thought gave me some uneasiness as
I hurried on my way.

In about half an hour I came in sight of a large
white mansion, just off the highway, standing in
the midst of handsome and commodious grounds.
From the entrance gate a broad graveled walk, or
drive, as it must have been in former days, led up to
the door, and the grounds were filled with flowers,
shrubbery, and hoary shade trees. A thick growth
of bright green Bermuda grass carpeted the earth
from the whitewashed fence to the house, affording
a delightful playground for several children who were
romping near the mansion. The house itself was
large, old fashioned and roomy—in many respects
a typical old Southern homestead of the bygone *régime* and which had probably been in the family for
many years.

I entered boldly. A wide and roomy piazza ran
the whole length of the house in front; and as I
drew near I perceived a dozen or more handsomely
dressed young people seated about it in various positions, engaged in animated conversation, their gay
young voices ringing out in merriest laughter from
time to time. Some pretty young misses were
reclining with practiced grace in parti-colored ham-

mocks, attended closely by gay cavaliers. As I approached this merry group I could not help contrast-
ing my own mean, coarse, and almost ragged attire
with their own; my large, rough, and ill-fitting shoes
with their polished boots; my unshorn and sun-black-
ened face with their delicate ones; and to feel that
my external appearance, in the eyes of such as they,
was very much against me.

Yet, hoping to receive just treatment at least, I
did not turn back. I ascended the broad steps and
walked across the piazza. It was only when I was
almost upon them that the animated group became
aware of me. Some of the party honored me with
supercilious glances, while the majority, especially
the young maidens, seemed to feel that in me they
beheld the representative of an unknown species of
the genus homo, or a queer nondescript.

A servant at this moment passed me, and I asked
to see Mr. Johnson. Mr. Johnson was not at home.
I then demanded to see the lady of the house, and
the servant stepped briskly away. Mrs. Johnson
came presently; and standing in a distant door
(which obliged me to speak in such a bawl that I
quite lifted the roof, and drew upon myself the indignant glances of the young ladies) she curtly inquired
what I wanted. Some of the young gentleman looked
up in contemptuous amusement as I replied that I
was in search of a place at which to stop for the night.

The lady informed me, in the fewest and curtest
terms, that she had as much company as she had
room for, hence I must look elsewhere for lodging.

Having thus spoken, she turned about and coolly walked away. I felt at the moment that had I arrived in a coach and four, and were my clothes of the latest French diagonal, my hat silk, and my shirt fine linen, I should have been courteously received and treated with elegant hospitality. But the fact remained, however, that the door had been shut, as it were, in my face; and for a moment I was so angry that I gave free expression to my feelings—rather more free, I fear, than the occasion demanded. I said, among other things, that I considered it a shame and an outrage to thus turn a fellow-being away from a door, under such circumstances, in a Christian country, and that it seemed to me scarcely less than a slander on civilization and the Christian religion.

When I had spoken in this manner, one of the young gentlemen present rose from his chair, and approached me, demanded in a tone of half-languid amusement:

"Are you a preacher, my friend?"

"No, sir," I returned, "I am not."

He seemed disappointed, and mused a moment with head bent down. Then a bright idea seemed to cross his mind, and he spoke with some eagerness.

"My friend," he said, "I will make you a proposition. If you will agree to hold prayer for us this evening, and will pray for us all, I will undertake to see that you get accommodated for the night. What do you say?"

This proposition seemed to amuse the other young people very much, and to meet with their full approval.

"Say yes, old gentleman," several of the young
ladies called out, laughing heartily, and becoming
more noisy than ever.

My first impulse was to give the first speaker a
token of my physical prowess, and go upon my way.
Then I reflected that by remaining and accepting
the insolent proposition of the young pagan, perhaps
I might be enabled to treat them to an entertain-
ment very different from the monkey-show they
seemed to expect. This resolution formed, I said to
him that I would do as he wished. He expressed his
satisfaction, the company applauded, and the young
man went in search of his "aunt" as he called the
lady of the house; coming back after a while to say
that his aunt had consented for me to remain.

Thereupon I walked down the piazza to its lowest
end in order to be away from the gay and obstreperous crowd and sat down. I remained here in undis-
turbed quiet, gazing about at the wide landscape
presented to my view—over which the early shades
of night were now descending—and reflecting upon
the incidents of my journey until supper was announced. The other occupants of the piazza paid
no further attention to me, and seemed to forget my
existence. When the evening meal was ready I was
shown into the dining-room and given a seat along
with the crowd of noisy young people. The meal
was splendid and delightful, the service elegant and
faultless. I was left entirely to my own devices, and
no notice whatever was taken of me. This enabled
me to satisfy in peace the keen appetite that a day's
travel had put an edge upon.

As we were rising from the table half an hour later
the master of the house came in; and his attention
being directed to the meanly-dressed stranger, he
honored me with a broad stare. I repaired to my
seat upon the piazza and remained there for some
hours. The night was pleasantly warm and a half-
moon shed her dim rays over the world. Presently
I heard the twang, thump, and other preliminary
sounds, as the strings of some musical instruments
were struck, which seemed to announce the beginning of a concert. Then the clear sweet notes of
some old melody rose upon the air, and the brooding
stillness of night was broken by the sound of merry
voices, light laughter, and the measured tread of
dancing feet. This was soon changed to polkas,
waltzes, and so on through the whole gamut of fash-
ionable dances. After midnight the music ceased;
the musicians departed, twanging their instruments
noisily as they went; the dancers left the ball-room,
and something like silence fell upon the house.

Some of the couples came out upon the piazza in
the moonlight, while others wandered about the
grounds in the falling dew, and many lingered about
the parlors. One couple promenading in the moonlight passed near me, and I heard the lady crying
out to her escort:

"Oh, Tom, just think! We haven't heard that
old gentleman pray for us yet!"

"No, by thunder!" answered a masculine voice.
"But we shall, by all the gods, big and little. Come
on, Kitty; I will leave you in the parlor, and go
hunt him up."

They turned and came on up the steps, her costly robes rustling over the polished floor, talking gayly but in subdued tones. They did not see me, sitting in the shadow near enough to touch them as they passed, conversing in confidential whispers, and so passing on out of sight. A moment after I heard the gay young pagan's voice as he went about bidding the guests assemble for prayer—which word he pronounced in anything but a reverent tone; and then I heard him asking for me. He stepped out upon the piazza calling for me as he came, and I rose from my seat and answered. He hastened forward at once, seizing me by the arm, and we entered the parlor together.

The family and guests were all assembled, the latter making very merry in a corner by themselves. The master of the house looked at me curiously as I entered, but he said nothing. My companion, still retaining his grasp upon my arm, paused in the center of the room (I detected him winking comically at the gay crowd in the corner, which almost convulsed them with suppressed mirth) and, with a low bow, spoke to the following purpose in a canting and sniffling tone:

"My dearly beloved brethren and sisters, and the congregation generally, we will now have divine service, conducted by the good brother here, during which you will please be silent, observing proper decorum, and—and—" here he paused, as if seeking to find a fitting climax to an impressive sentence, and finally added in his natural voice: "and—and— *behave* yourselves."

This sally, which depended upon the manner of the speaker, rather than upon any words he might say for its humorous effect, was greeted with shouts of laughter, and my companion released his hold upon my arm, and took his seat among the younger portion of the company. Every eye was then turned expectantly upon me, and my first act was to call for a Bible. Those present seemed surprised at this; but a Bible was promptly brought, and I opened it, seated myself in such a manner as to face them all, and read a few extracts that made the cheeks of the young sinners tingle with shame. Seeing the effect I had produced, I closed the Bible, knelt down, and humbly offered a prayer to the Most High. It is not necessary to repeat that petition here, nor any part of it; it suffices to say that I had fully determined to touch the hearts of my hearers, and appeal to their better natures; and my task was so far accomplished that when I rose from my knees there was hardly a pair of dry eyes in the room.

The thoughtless young people—whose levity, like that of many others, was entirely on the surface—immediately crowded round me to grasp my hand and ask my pardon, which, you may be sure, was very willingly granted. Mr. and Mrs. Johnson were very much affected, and it seemed as though they could not do me honor enough. During the time I remained with them they treated me with distinguished courtesy, and pressed me to stop indefinitely with them. My victory was complete; and the young ladies and young gentlemen learned, perhaps for the first time in their lives, that a human heart, with a human capacity for love, kindness, and shrinking from humiliation, might be found under the coarsest homespun coat.

When I resumed my journey next day, Mrs. Johnson prepared for me a lunch that would have delighted an epicure, and which was sufficient for half a dozen men. I took leave of them with much regret, nor do I ever think of them save with the greatest good-will and esteem.

It was shortly after this that certain symptoms, which had been troubling me for some time, became more pronounced. I suffered from excessive and continual thirst, and my appetite came and went in the most extraordinary and capricious manner. I suffered at times from a feeling of great weakness, and from soreness and pain in the limbs. My weight became very much reduced, and at intervals a feeling of the most terrible depression and melancholy came over me. Yet these symptoms would sometimes abate or almost wholly disappear for days at a time. Again they would increase in violence, and there were other symptoms far more alarming than those that have been mentioned.

I traveled as rapidly as possible, and there were days in which I walked long distances, while in others my physical weakness, which seemed to gradually increase, was so urgent that traveling was only accomplished at the expense of intense suffering. I did not then know what was the matter with me. It was only when I placed myself under the treatment of a distinguished physician that I learned the awful truth that I was afflicted with Diabetes Mellitus* in its worst and most malignant form. I was warned at the time that the disease was incurable.

My eyesight became affected and grew steadily worse. I found at times that I could scarcely see at all, and for a few days before reaching Berwick's Bay I experienced the terrible and .helpless feeling of seeing the ground on which I walked suddenly rising in great wave like rolls before me, and sinking as suddenly into deep pits and depressions. It rose in ridges and hollows very much like waves at sea; and often, in raising my foot to step upon a ridge half as high as my head, which would suddenly appear in the smooth road before me, I would find it descending into a pit-like depression. As a .consequence I found myself at times staggering like a drunken man; and I do not doubt that anyone who chanced to see me walking in this uncertain manner over roads that must have appeared perfectly smooth to him, considered me as a drunkard. This distressing symptom continued with varying intensity until I reached Berwick's Bay, and hence my traveling was necessarily much slower than it had been.

It was several weeks—I do not remember how

* "In Diabetes Mellitus the mind is often greatly altered; depression of spirits, decline in firmness of character and moral tone, with irritability and defects of vision are present."

"*The Blood and various secretions contain sugar.*"

"The majority of cases prove fatal. The prognosis is most unfavorable * * * it being fairly questionable if complete recovery has ever taken place."—From Dr. Hughes' "*Practice.*"

many—from the time of my escape from the asylum that I arrived at Berwick's Bay. On reaching this place, which is also called Morgan City, I made search for a quiet boarding-place, finally selecting that kept by a Mrs. Smith. This lady was a widow, and was so kind to me during my stay that I shall always think of her with the deepest gratitude and esteem.

And now my eyesight, instead of improving, as I had fondly hoped it would, became steadily worse, and I became very much alarmed. But as nothing could be done under the circumstances, I merely waited, trusting that the disease would in time get better or entirely leave me.

One morning, however, a few days after my arrival, when I woke, as I usually did about sunrise, every thing about me was wrapped in Stygian darkness. Supposing that for some reason I had awakened at an earlier hour than usual, I turned over and went to sleep. In the course of an hour or two, or perhaps more, I woke again; yet still all was dark. Wondering in a vague way what the trouble was, I left my bed, and after some trouble, succeeded in dressing myself. I then felt about in search of a match, and I soon found one and struck it. It made a loud noise, as parlor matches do, and I heard the tiny blaze flare up. *Heard*, but did not see. The match was burning brightly—there could be no doubt of that, for I could plainly hear the spluttering of the flame as it ran up the bit of wood. Yet the same rayless blackness reigned around me.

Then the truth came home to me—came with such force and terrible intensity that I staggered and would have fallen had I not touched the wall. *I was blind!* Without an instant's warning or a moment's notice hopeless darkness had come upon me.

I fell upon my knees in the darkness, and mumbled out some incoherent words—tried to pray. The maddening rush of feeling—the anguish—the despair —the utter hopelessness, and the horror of the moment, can never be described. I tried to pray, but could not. Words would not come—only a senseless muttering; and so, overwhelmed with despair and speechless anguish, I lay prone upon the floor. In this state I lay for some time; but there finally came a knock at my door—though I heard it not; and in the unaccountable silence which followed, Mrs. Smith became alarmed and opened the door.

"Mr. Nall! Mr. Nall!" she cried, in frightened accents, seeing the position in which I lay upon the floor.

Her cry broke the spell. I knew her voice, and knew by the rush of air that my door stood open, yet all was Egyptian blackness.

"Mr. Nall," she faltered, "what is the matter?"

Turning my sightless eyes upon her, and raising my hands on high, I groaned in accents of hopeless despair:

"Mrs. Smith, I—I—I am blind!"

"Blind!" she cried, in horror. "Blind! Oh Mr. Nall!"

"Blind—yes blind! I cannot see—I hear, but

cannot see you. All is dark—blacker than night!"
"Great God!" she exclaimed, stepping back. "How
horrible!" and she began to weep.

Almost stupefied with despair, I was hardly conscious that she was weeping. Disease had so sapped
my physical energies and taken my strength that I
did not have the fortitude, the manly resolution,
that I would have had otherwise, to bear my affliction
calmly. At this moment, from bodily weakness or
other causes I became unconscious, and when I came
to my senses I heard male and female voices near me,
and could feel that I no longer lay upon the floor. I
attempted to rise, but a hand pressed me back, and
a masculine voice exclaimed, kindly but firmly:

"No, no, Mr. Nall; do not attempt to rise, as you
would only fall. We have moved you down here in
the sitting room, and seated you in a large rocking-
chair."

They then—the gentleman being a physician
whom they had sent for in great haste when I fell
swooning to the floor—talked to me kindly and encouragingly, with the evident intention of drawing
my mind away from gloomy or despairing reflections.
But such was the feeling of cold despair tugging at
my heart-strings that I scarce minded what they said.

Presently the physician spoke:

"Now, Mr. Nall, do try to rouse yourself from this
lethargy of despair. No good can come of it, my
word for it. I realize that the misfortune seems
much more terrible to you than it would if you were
in better health or among your relatives; but you

owe it to your God to try and rouse yourself. Your blindness may only be—and probably is—temporary, and your sight may possibly return as suddenly as it went. Try to rouse yourself."

These words were heartily spoken and kindly meant; but as is usual in such cases, they had little effect. Indeed, what he asked was impossible. My misfortune had come upon me with such terrible and fatal swiftness, and meant so much to me, that I earnestly prayed for death. My sufferings had been so dreadful, I had borne so much, and been afflicted so long, that now, when the mists had lifted, and the shadows were rolling from me, it seemd very hard to have the full goblet snatched from my eager lips and dashed to the earth. While these thoughts were passing through my mind the physician was preparing to take his leave   I heard his footsteps and those of Mrs. Smith as they turned to leave the room. To be left entirely alone with my darkness and my despair was a thought I could not bear.

"Don't leave me!" I cried to them. "For the love of heaven don't leave me alone in this terrible darkness   I should die! I cannot bear the thought."

In my agitation I sprang up and advanced 'a few steps towards them, but so great was the feeling of helplessness which possessed me that I fell to the floor.

They ran to me hastily and lifted me back to my chair.

"His blindness has come upon him so suddenly at a time of great weakness and prostration from disease, and it is such an unaccustomed experience to him that he has a horror of being left alone," said the doctor, in a low voice; "and really," he continued, "just now he is more helpless than an infant. Of course he will gradually become more accustomed to it, and will to a great extent lose that feeling of utter helplessness which is so distressing to him now."

"I will not leave you, Mr. Nall," said Mrs. Smith, her kind heart touched by my need. "The doctor will have to go, but I will sit with you until I am compelled to go about my duties, and I will then get some one to stay with you."

She then sat down in a chair near at hand.

I thanked her; and touched by her disinterested kindness, and are vulsion of feeling now coming over me, I could not restrain my tears. Growing calmer after a moment, and soothed by the knowledge that I had the sympathy of one good heart, my misfortune took on a newer and less hopeless aspect, and for some hours I felt more cheerful and resigned.

In the afternoon I sent for one of the officials of the local Masonic lodge—of which Society I had been a life-long member—and giving him a partial account of my history and condition—as much as was proper and necessary for him to know—that noble Order now came to my relief. The necessary funds were subscribed, my lodging paid, and a boy employed to remain with me night and day. It will thus be seen that had I not been a member of that ancient and beneficent Order I should have perished.

After a few days, as the physician had predicted,

I could submit to being led about without feeling every instant that I should fall. Leaning upon the arm of my attendant I walked about the house, and for the exercise so badly needed, promenaded the yard.

While all these things made my lot much easier to bear, my depression and melancholy were very great, and I sincerely longed for death. The gloom that haunted me was profound, and had I possessed the means I should unhesitatingly have taken my own life. Doubtless, however, my kind friends entertained some suspicion as to how matters stood, and my attendant never left me for a moment.

As a means of diverting my mind from these gloomy reflections, as well as with the design of passing my time more agreeably, I expressed a wish to write some articles if anyone would undertake the office of amanuensis. For this difficult task the kind-hearted Mrs. Smith volunteered her services; and the result of our collaboration was a series of articles entitled "*A Way-Worn-Traveler.*" They were published in the New Orleans *Times-Democrat;* and Mrs Smith was so affected by them that she gave me a little purse containing two dollars and fifty cents in silver and urged me to accept it. After some hesitation I did so, having a special use for it, as the reader shall see.

Supplied now by the kindness of Mrs. Smith with the sum mentioned, I thought I saw a way to escape my misery. Relapsing again into gloom and despondency terrible in their intensity, and feeling that joy and love and "mortal faith" had gone from me forever, does it seem strange that I now sought death?

The means were not far to seek. The bayou, silent and swift, hastened on toward the sea a short distance away; and I knew that under its dark waters, as under the tide of ancient Lethe, unbroken rest and forgetfulness awaited me. Death and the grave, thoughts which are harrowing and gruesome in health and spirits, no longer had any terrors for me; and I knew that once beneath the changing tide of the bayou, all would be ended.

I realized, however, the impossibility of getting away from my attendant. Even had I been able to do so I could never make my way to the bayou unaided, and no stranger I might meet would assist me, for to the simple question: "What can a blind man want on the banks of a deep swift river?" what could I say?

Obviously, some other course was necessary. I must persuade or bribe my attendant to accompany me to the stream if I ever meant to reach it. But this, as I soon ascertained, was not easy to do. Neither money nor entreaties would induce him to violate his orders. He had, he said, the most positive instructions not to allow me to go beyond the yard gate; and though I begged him most earnestly and offered him all the money I had about me, he remained unmoved.

"No, Mr. Nall," the faithful boy would say, "I would like to do what you ask, but," here he would shake his head, "I can't because I promised them I wouldn't."

"But Charley," I would urge, with great earnestness, "you might take me, if you only would, for a moment—just for a moment."

"No, sir," was the firm reply, "I cannot."

"Only for a moment," was my constant entreaty, "I want to go down to the river side just for a moment to—to see—to find whether I can see the boats come in."

"As a matter of fact, I well knew that I could not see the boats come in, or go out, or come or go at all. My blindness was so absolute that I could not, as many blind persons can do, distinguish between day and night. I could not see the least gleam of light when I held my face toward the sun at midday, and even when a brightly burning torch was held within a foot of my eyes I could see nothing but the most absolute darkness.

But I know now, as I might have realized then, that my pretense of wanting to "see the boats come in" was too shallow to deceive even a child. It did not possess even the doubtful merit of plausibility, and the boy understood my purpose as certainly as though I had told him in so many words that I meant to drown myself, and he was even more careful than before that I did not leave the yard.

I was under the necessity, therefore, of foregoing my design; and I finally ceased to urge my attendant to become unfaithful to his trust. As soon as I understood that there was no chance for the execution of my purpose, almost as by magic I became less despondent and melancholy, and I resolved to make the

best of matters as they stood.   From this time forward my burden did not press so heavily upon me.

Yet whenever I thought of the weary years stretching out before me, I knew not how many nor how
long, where I had fondly looked forward to a participation in many of the joys of life; and when mortal
disease had fastened its fangs upon me, I felt indeed
that the doom of blindness had brought upon me an
"Iliad of woes."

I remained in a state of total blindness for more
than five-and-forty days.   There would have been
some comfort—though ever so little—in the thought
that I could distinguish night from day; but this
was denied me, and night and day were as one.

One morning towards the middle of the second
month I woke as usual, a while before the breakfast
hour.   The morning sun was shining brightly in
through the uncurtained window, filling the room
with light.   For a moment I failed to realize what
such an ordinary sight meant to me.   Then I struggled hastily to a sitting posture and gazed at the sun-
light like a man demented.   Wonder, joy, incredulity,
and heart-felt thankfulness were each contending
for the mastery; and throwing back the cover I started
to spring from the bed, but fell back, for a moment,
upon the sheets.   As suddenly as blindness had come
upon me—without warning and without notice, my
eyesight had returned.   Not wholly.   Yet all—nay,
more than I could ask for.   I sprang up in the wild-
ness of joy which now rushed over me, and seizing

my garments with trembling hands, attempted to dress, but threw them aside the next instant and ran to the window. My eyes were blurred with tears, yet I could see the fair green earth smiling before me. Rushing back I threw myself face downward upon the bed and prayed aloud.

The restoration of my eyesight was not complete, and even to this day—in the soft winds and fragrant breezes of the spring of 1893—it is imperfect, and I do not see well; but the terrible experiences of my two months' blindness remain yet fresh in my memory—vivid as though the obscuring mists of time had rolled away, and I stood once more upon the banks of Berwick's Bay, blind and helpless.

In the meantime physical weakness had grown upon me to so alarming an extent that I could not have traveled on foot a dozen miles in a day. A perpetual feeling of coldness haunted me, and in the air of night, which was only pleasant to others, my teeth chattered with cold. A local physician advised me to go to a distinguished surgeon at San Antonio, Texas. The climate at that point was genial, and would in itself no doubt greatly benefit me. He impressed upon my mind the fact that this was my only hope. But how could I get to San Antonio? I had no means, and was no longer able to walk, and how then could I get to the eminent practitioner who could probably save my life?

After a few days of cogitation I formulated a plan —desperate, indeed, and wicked, but still a plan—

by which I could supply myself with the funds necessary for my trip. As a preliminry step I left Berwick's Bay and went half a score of miles further into the interior of the country. This brought me into a section inhabited chiefly by negroes, and these were ignorant, credulous, and reeking with superstition and filth. I sought out one of their most popular preachers, a pompous old black, swelled with dignity and self-importance.

I then told him, after some complimentary and flattering remarks, which made him swell all the more, that I was representing a great Chicago publishing firm (whose name I did *not* give) who wished to present a handsome Bible to every worthy negro; that the Bible was given free; but that for the sum of twenty-five cents we would print the owner's name in large gold characters on the back. I told him further that I wanted his assistance and his advice as to the best method of giving every worthy darkey a chance to secure a magnificent Bible.

The sable minister fell in with the scheme readily; gave me twenty-five cents upon the spot; and said that he wanted his full name in large letters on his Bible—George Washington Abraham Lincoln Esau Johnson Jacob Jones. This lengthy name he insisted on having set down in full, and he impressed upon me the fact that the letters were to be large.

He watched me with much satisfaction as I wrote down this unique name; and when I had done, he told me that as the next day was Sunday he would call his flock together, and no doubt I would find that everyone would want a Bible.

True to his promise he assembled his congregation on the following morning. When all had arrived he rose in his pulpit and explained to them the nature of my business, and advised them all to come forward with the money and make application for a Bible.

The preacher had hardly concluded his remarks when the dusky congregation began to crowd forward with more eagerness than politeness, by twos, threes, and by dozens, and finally all together—of all ages, sexes, sizes and conditions;—scrambling, pushing, the silly ones tittering loudly in many keys, the impatient ones muttering curses, and all combining to form a scene one would hardly care to see repeated. For the next hour or so I was kept busy writing down names (some of them the most absurb that ever were heard of) and receiving money. Many of the negroes had no cash with them, but with true African impulsiveness all such borrowed it from their more fortunate brothers upon the spot and paid it over to me. When the last silver-piece was handed in, I counted the names upon my list and found that it ran up to something more than a hundred.

I then secured a recommendation from the Rev. G. W. A. L. E. J. J. Jones, and went on further into the country. I sought out another preacher, explained the nature of my business to him, and gave him the recommendation I had secured from his brother expounder of moral law, whom he happened to know. In this manner I passed more than a week going about among the negroes from place to place until I had got together the sum of $57.00. During

this time I suffered very much from cold, though to
others the weather was only pleasantly warm, and
my chilled frame, weak and painful eyes, and puny
strength gave me no little trouble. I adopted all
manner of artifices to instill a little fugitive warmth
into my shivering body, some of which were successful, while others were not. I could not conceal from
myself the disagreeable truth that I had become a
confirmed—nay, and well nigh a helpless, valetudi-
narian.

My peregrinations led me at this time through a
prairie country. Some of the streams I came to
were wooded, while others ran through a bare and
open district, destitute of forests or trees. The leading industry was sugar-making. One evening just
after nightfall, after a day of unusual bodily suffering, I came, while attempting to walk a mile or two,
which was an effort too great for my strength, upon
a huge sugar-boiler near a small collection of country
houses. The fires which had been left in the furnace
earlier in the evening had now smouldered to ashes,
and a warmth, at once life giving and pleasant to an
exhausted frame like mine, was all that remained of
the intense heat of a few hours before. A number
of small huts were standing near, but no human being,
so far as I could see, was in the vicinity. I thereupon climbed up and laid my chilled and shivering
body at full length upon the top of the boiler, and
in a few moments experienced such a grateful and
drowsy glow of gentle heat steal over my tired frame
that I felt myself sinking into a pleasant and soothing

state of half sleep. A bright half moon had been shedding her rays over the wide and level landscape, but now she went out of sight behind a huge drift of cloud which was banked against the southern sky. An increased drowsiness crept over me, and every conscious sensation of pleasure or of pain was lost in the deep calm of sleep. I slept quietly, as I knew afterwards, the whole night through, and might have remained unconscious upon the boiler until far up into the day, had I not been rudely interrupted just as the first glances of the sun were peeping over the eastern hills. I felt myself jerked, with more violence than gentleness from my comfortable position, and a rude voice exclaimed:

"You gits down from hier. You coomes mit me."

I felt myself slipping, with more speed than grace, from the boiler to the ground. As soon as my feet reached terra firma I saw before me the squat, almost shapeless figure of a low-browed Dutchman, dressed in coarse, scanty, and ill-fitting clothes, and possessed of a broad red face that was dull, stupid and phlegmatic.

"Vat do you mean—" he began, as my feet touched the ground.

"What do you mean, you pragmatic Dutch villain," I struck in, angrily, "pulling at me in such a manner?"

"Vat beezness had you on dot b'iler?" he demanded, in a blustering manner, but stepping back beyond my reach as he spoke.

"Business enough to teach you a lesson," I retorted, "if you don't keep a more civil tongue in your head."

And then, without waiting for a reply, which I did not care to hear, I went on my way without more ado.

On the following day, while standing, near the noon hour, among a collection of miserable shanties where a number of sugar-workers were hurrying to and fro on their various duties, I saw a small newspaper lying on a table near at hand. I picked it up and glanced through its columns. I think the name of this paper was the *Teche Pilot*, a country journal issued that day or the day before. I turned over the pages indifferently and the reader may judge my surprise when I found my attention arrested by the following:

"HANG THE SCOUNDREL!"

"We have lately received information to the effect that a man named Nall is traveling through some parts of this parish victimizing the negroes by pretending to sell them Bibles for 25 cents. Of course the negro who is fool enough to part with his money never sees it or the man again. Nall seems to have made considerable money by his rascality. The good white people of this parish should catch the scoundrel and tar-and-feather or hang him. A man who goes among the negroes in this manner, cheating them out of their money, and who thus takes away from the parish so much of the money which should be spent in patronizing home institutions, should be killed."

I read this precious outburst—which I thought revealed the cloven foot in the last sentence—carefully through. I then put the paper back where I got it, and started, as I had determined the previous day to do, for the nearest railroad station. I had secured the money to pay for the treatment of a distinguished physician,* and had thus acccomplished my object, and was satisfied. I did not return to Berwick's Bay, but purchased a railway ticket and started on my journey to San Antonio. This place was the home of the celebrated Dr. Herf, and if medical skill could save me—this with apologies to "those advertising doctors," who cure everything—I knew that I could rely upon Dr. Herf.

Who was it that said, and has the world justified the saying, that *necessitas non habet legem!*

* As this statement may not appear very clear to the reader, the following explanation is offered. As a matter of fact $50.00 would *not* pay for the treatment of an eminent physician in a difficult case, nor probably even the fifth part of it. The members of the medical profession are daily performing more acts of charity, more deeds of goodness, which are never known to the public at large, and for which they receive no credit, or perhaps even thanks, than any other class of men. When called upon to treat a difficult case, without the hope of pay for his services, the physician does not hesitate, but freely gives the patient the benefit of his whole skill and experience. And I may add that in many cases he gets only abuse: or ingratitude at the least, for his pains. For these reasons I knew that the San Antonio physician would treat me—would promptly and cheerfully do his best for me when his time was more valuable than gold, even though he *knew* that I had no money at all, and would *never* have.

CHAPTER VIII.

"YOU HAVE A DISEASE THAT WILL KILL YOU."

Adversity's cold frosts will soon be over.　　　　　*Hemans.*

Man, proud man
Drest in a little brief authority,
Most ignorant of what he's most assured,
His glassy essence, like an angry ape,
Plays such fantastic tricks before high heaven
As makes the angels weep.　　　　　*Shakespeare.*

Borne swiftly as steam could take me from the
scenes of my recent exploits, I thought with wonder
of the almost miraculous events that had lately
occurred to me. Of my escape from perpetual darkness I thought with gratitude and awe; and of the
kind friends who had so generously and ungrudgingly
come forward to assist me in my hour of sore distress
I thought with a variety of feelings impossible to
describe. It seemed to me now, in the light of
recent occurrences, that I had not in the past been
sufficiently grateful for the few blessings that had
been left me, and I resolved that in the future, so
long as the inestimable boon of sight were spared
me, I should look upon myself as being a favorite of
fortune. Thus do great misfortunes, and the loss of
that which we, so long as we possessed it, lightly

164

prized, make us understand and appreciate and be thankful for the few gifts that remain.

I stopped first at the town of Beaumont, in the neighboring State of Texas. This town was situated not far from the coast, in the midst of an extensive belt of long-leaf pines. Hence lumber-making is the principal industry. I had a brother here, younger than myself, whom I wished to see. I need hardly say that I approached him very circumspectly, as I did not know whether, actuated by mistaken kindness, he might not attempt to communicate with the asylum authorities with the purpose of having me sent back to the hospital. This fear, as the reader has no doubt learned, had become, so to speak, the nightmare of my existence, and it continued to be so for some time to come. Indeed, until I reached the Pacific coast, the names I used, and gave as my own, were pseudonyms always.

With these feelings uppermost in my mind, I put my brother under vows of secrecy before making known my purposes or destination. This done, we conversed very freely, and I remained with him for some days. On parting from him I went immediately to San Antonio in order to get the benefit of the celebrated Dr. Herf's treatment and advice.

Down on Commerce Street there was a hostelry which went under the name (let us say) of the Cleveland House. It was at this place that I stopped. A Mrs. Hanna (we shall call her thus, though it was not her name) was the ostensible or nominal proprietress. Her husband, Mr. Hanna, was the real owner. But Mr. Hanna was also the proprietor of a café near the "Sunset" depot, and passed most of his time there. He came over to the Cleveland House almost every day (never at night) and made things unpleasant for a few hours, for he was not a genial man. As soon as I had completed arrangements with Mrs. Hanna I called at the offices of Dr. Herf.

On the occasion of my first visit he interrogated me closely, and examined me with great care, and to the question which had been burning on my tongue for I know not how long, "What do you think is the matter with me?" he did not answer directly, but told me to come back at that hour on the following day.

"It is impossible," he said, by way of explanation, as I turned to depart, "for reasons which you will no doubt understand, for me to give you a positive opinion now, and any other kind of opinion would be worth nothing to you."

My eagerness to hear his diagnosis of my case was so great that on the day following, at the same hour, I was knocking at his door. As soon as I found myself in his presence I put my question for the second time, but more eagerly, if possible, than before. This time he answered me with a question of his own.

"Have you a family, Mr. Nall?"

This interrogatory, while it surprised and even alarmed me, I answered in the briefest terms.

"Well," said he, when he had heard my reply, "you had better go to them."

Greatly surprised and alarmed, as much from his

manner and tone as from his words, I asked: "What do you mean?"

"I mean," he responded, in a kind tone, "that you ought to be with your family because of the nature of your disease, which, not to keep you in suspense, is Diabetes Mellitus in an aggravated form."

This was a disease I had never heard of, and knew nothing about, hence I did not know whether to be frightened or not. Before I could put my thoughts into words, Dr. Herf continued:

"I speak thus plainly," said he, "because I believe that you have too much manhood and courage to want me to delude you with false hopes, or misrepresent your true condition."

"Is this disease, then," said I, "so serious as that?"

He hesitated a moment (for though he was too sincere a man to mislead me, even in trifles, yet he had little of that brutal frankness so common among some physicians) and replied:

"I regret that my duty compels me to say to you that it is incurable, and that sooner or later it will kill you."

When he had thus spoken my doom, in these brief words, a dead silence fell upon us, and neither of us cared to break it.

"But, doctor," said I at length, "if I prefer to remain here in the city, instead of returning to my home, the very idea of which is repugnant to me for many reasons, will you take charge of my case and do what you can for me?"

"Yes," he answered, "I will."

I did remain for some time, and went regularly to the offices of the distinguished physician, and although he had warned me at the outset that he could not *cure* the disease with which I was afflicted, yet his treatment benefited me very greatly and no doubt kept me from taking to my bed (from which I should never have risen).

I continued thus for something more than a month, at the end of which time my slender stock of money gave entirely out. In the meantime, having written to my brother, Mr. James B. Fleming, at Beaumont, I learned that he was dead—had died suddenly of a malignant attack of pneumonia within a few days after I had left him. Thus, having neither money nor the means of earning it, I entered into an agreement with my landlady to perform certain duties for her house, in return for which I was to receive board and lodging for another month. Thus I got along very well.

One afternoon shortly after I had thus begun I was standing upon the platform of one of the city depots when I observed a muscular-looking mulatto negro gazing at me in a very fixed and significant manner. This small circumstance made me somewhat uneasy, laboring, as I constantly did, under the fear of detection and apprehension. Hence I avoided old acquaintances as much as possible, and had a morbid dread of being recognized by anyone. The negro just mentioned was large and muscular. From his towering height I judged that he must have stood more than six feet in his shoes. His complexion was rather dark for a mulatto, and his hair long and very woolly. No sooner had I observed this fixed gaze at me than I drew my hat further down over my eyes, and shrank back into the shadow as much as possible. This manœuvre, however, did not have the desired effect. On the contrary it served only to increase the suspicion with which the black already regarded me. He did not therefore cease or mitigate his annoying espionage, but changed his position from time to time, and I think surveyed me from every point of the compass. Presently, with a broad grin of delight upon his face—which, though it was a homely, was an honest one—he crossed over to where I stood, and still grinning, said:

"Am dat Mr. Flunggins?"

"No," I replied, firmly, "my name is Nall."

A shade of disappointment, mingled with regret and doubt, crossed his face. He stepped back, but still gazed at me.

I could see that he wished to question me, but I had determined to give him no encouragement. On the contrary I resolved to adopt a different course. Finding such surveillance anything but agreeable, and seeing, too, that I had not entirely deceived him, I stepped forward, threw back my hat, and told him fiercely to go about his business, and leave off his impertinent stare, or I should chastise him upon the spot. At this he fell back to his former position without making any reply; but I saw that he knew me, and I resolved to return to my hotel by the most circuitous route I could think of. I thereupon started hastily up the street. The negro followed me immediately, but made no further attempt to speak. It was only, however, the fear of personal violence which kept him at a distance, and fearing that in his blind affection he would cause me annoyance in the future, I paused before going many blocks and permitted him to come up with me. When he saw that I had paused, he appeared to hardly know whether to advance or not, as he had evidently not forgotten my threat. I called out to him encouragingly, and he came up to me without any sign of fear.

"Mr. Flunggins," said this persistent black, as he came up grinning," da'ts you—I *knows* dat's you. You aint no Nall. No, sah," he continued, shaking his head knowingly," you caint fool dis nigger."

"Possibly I resemble someone you have known," said I.

"No, sah, Mahse Mac, I knows dat ar vois—dis yere nigger *knows* yer. Doan' you know *me?* Doan' you ricerlic Dick—yo' ole nigger Dick?"

"Yes, Dick," I answered, giving him the hand he had been so longing to grasp, "I do remember you," and the negro, delighted, cut so many antics and capers about the street that the passers-by gazed at us curiously.

I talked with the faithful old black for some hours, and gave him a brief account of many of the incidents related in these pages. Many years before he had been a servant in our family, and had remembered us all with gratitude and affection. At my request he wrote certain letters, an account of which is given in Chapter III.

After which I saw him quite frequently during the time I remained in San Antonio. He had a small restaurant down on some by-street, and at his urgent and oft-repeated request I went there occasionally. As to the work I performed for the landlady of the Cleveland House, she expressed herself as being well pleased. But on one evil day I brought in a guest—a nicely-dressed stranger claiming to be from Sedalia, who was destined to do me much harm—indeed, to be the means of starting me again on my wanderings. A gentleman he appeared to be, and he had a pleasing way that took well with all, especially with the ladies. He walked with me from the depot to the house I represented, in the most condescending manner, and as soon as we reached the office, he expressed a desire to speak with the landlady privately. In this conversation, as I afterwards ascertained, he spoke to her about as follows:

"My object, madam, in thus speaking to you is because I wish to deal frankly with you. In this spirit I will therefore say to you that at present I am entirely out of money. I have written home for a supply, but until this comes I must have some place at which to stay. If you will give me accommodations here you may be sure that when the money for which I have sent arrives I will pay your bill without question."

Some further conversation ensued, and Mrs. Hanna, finding him so persuasive, soft, gentle, and kindly-spoken, and courteous, that, unluckily for me, she took him in, gave him the best room in the house,

and treated him in every way with distinguished con-
sideration. Nay, more; carried away by the soft
flattery which he every day poured into her willing
ears, she discharged a servant whom she suspected
of having neglected to attend immediately to some
trivial order which her artful guest had given. He
remained with us for about ten days, and during that
time was toasted, *feted*, flattered and wined and dined
to his heart's content. Mrs. Hanna could not do
enough for him, and made a complete fool of herself
as long as he remained. But all of this came to an
abrupt end in a manner which astonished none of us
but the landlady herself. One night when we all
slumbered and slept, our stranger gathered together
his worldly possessions, stealthily raised his bed-room
window, and we never saw him more.

When Mrs. Hanna learned that he had thus abruptly departed, and that he had not stopped nor
stayed even to bid her good-bye, she fell into a great
rage. Perhaps the consciousness that she had made
an entire fool of herself added fuel to her fury in no
small degree. At any rate the more she reflected
upon the incidents of the past week or so, the more
terrible grew her wrath. And woman-like, the
angrier she became, the more unreasonable, unjust,
and unreasoning she showed herself to be. As ill
fortune would have it, no one but myself was present
when her paroxysm reached its height, and she turned
upon me and poured out upon my head all the vials
of her wrath. The more I endeavored to reason
with her the more enraged and unreasonable she be-

came. Finally, after hurling at me every expletive or epithet of which she was mistress, or could coin for the occasion, she accused me of being in collusion with her departed guest.

"Why, madam," said I, determined to make some attempt at least to vindicate myself, "it was not I who made the arrangement with the gentleman—not I who took him in. I never saw him in all my life before, and had no means of knowing whether he had one dollar or a thousand. You took him in knowing he had no money."

"But you brought him here!" she shrieked "You brought him here, and what did you do it for, if it was not to cheat me out of my hard-earned money? For aught I know you helped him to sneak away in the night like a thief. You may have raised the window for him! I do not know but what you are a greater scoundrel than he is! And you can get out from here! You can leave here!"

"I am quite well aware, madam," returned I, angered at her unjust and unreasonable treatment of me, "that I *can* leave here. I *can*, I suppose, leave at any moment; but the question is, *will I?*"

With that I turned away and left her, and went up to my room, leaving her standing in the middle of the floor staring after me, fairly petrified with astonishment and indignation, and glaring with impotent rage. Presently I heard her walk hurriedly across the room and give a violent ring at the telephone bell. I paused on the stairway long enough to ascertain that the enraged woman was sending for her

husband, and then I went on up to my room. The
only baggage I had consisted of two large valises.
I packed my small belongings into them, and locked
them carefully. I then brushed my hair and started
to return to the office. On the way down I overtook
an Irishman who was a regular guest at the house,
and with whom I had formed a pleasant acquaint-
anceship from the first hour of my arrival. I never
knew his name. Everyone called him "Jim," and I
called him Jim. If he had any other name I never
knew it. He was a man in the prime of life, very
jolly, and very impulsive and warm-hearted. By
some lucky stroke in the railroad business he had
accumulated a modest fortune, and with this had
retired from active business life. I had liked him
from the first, and we had formed quite a friendship.
He often came to my room of evenings, and we would
smoke and pass the time in conversation and story-
telling until midnight. As I overtook him now on
the stairway, he smiled and said:

"What's the row?"

"Mrs. Hanna has become enraged at me because
her impecunious guest has departed without bidding
her good-bye," I replied; "and she wishes to lay the
blame of the whole affair upon me."

"Just like a woman," he growled, oracularly. (He
was an old bachelor, and like most old bachelors, he
understood, or thought he understood, all the little
weaknesses of the gentle sex.) "I heard her shrieking and howling a bit ago, and feared you were in
trouble with the old skinflint. Satan himself couldn't

get along with that woman. No, nor Christ, neither."

By this time we had reached the office and found it deserted. We sat down by the stove and continued our conversation. I kept my eye, however, upon the street door, as I did not know what moment Hanna might step in. I saw by the clock which ticked upon the wall near at hand that it was about four o'clock.

"I think, Jim," I said, "that madam has sent for her husband. At any rate I heard her at the telephone, and caught enough of what she said to be pretty sure that she has sent for him. She ordered me to leave, and I gave her a pretty broad hint that I would not do so. You see she agreed in the beginning to board me for one month, and that time has not yet elapsed."

"Well, Mr. Nall," said my friend, "you remain in the office here with me, until old Hanna comes, which I guess he'll do pretty soon, and if he insults you, why d— him, knock him down, and I'll stand by you."

As I thanked him for this impulsive mark of friendship, Hanna, followed by his wife, entered the room, and we could say no more. We saw at a glance that Hanna was very angry, and I had no means of knowing what his wife had told him. Judging by his angry looks, however, it must have been such a story as to discompose him very much. I felt sure that she had poured into his ears a woful and terrible tale of insults, injuries, etc. She looked at me with an expression of vindictive triumph as her lord strode angrily up to me, and extending his right arm towards me threateningly, exclaimed, in a harsh, angry, and imperious tone:

"You get out of this house, you scoundrel!"

I sat perfectly still, without making any reply, or appearing to notice him at all. Hanna rolled his angry eyes about the office for a moment, as if in search of something he did not see, and then turning to his wife, he told her to go up stairs and bring down "Nall's things."

She departed with alacrity, after giving me a mocking and insolent glance.

"You're a nice specimen of humanity!" said Hanna to me, in a coarse, brutal, and sneering tone, and my own anger rose so high that I curbed it with difficulty, and repressed the retort that rose to my lips. Then, as though satisfied with this, he said no more for the moment. I afterwards knew, however, that he took my silence at the moment as a clear sign of physical cowardice, or want of that personal or physical courage—the Anglo-Saxon *fighting instinct* —so greatly admired by most Texans, and so generally possessed by them. He waited a few moments and then returned to the attack with great volubility and energy.

I thereupon endeavored to reason with him, but everything I said merely served to throw fuel upon the flame of his wrath. He became even more unreasonable than his wife had been, and he had evidently tried and condemned me in his own mind without waiting or wishing to hear my statement of

the case.   It may have been, too, that his desire to
show his small authority, and, shielded by the law,
to browbeat and domineer, was greater than his
feeble faculties could resist.   He told me very loftily,
several times over, that I need not open my mouth,
or say a word, as he "knew me," and would not listen
to anything I said.

Presently his wife came slowly down the stairway
with my valises in her hand; and, panting with the
vigor of her exertions, but triumphant still, she
placed them upon the floor near her husband.   As
soon as this was done, she stepped to one side, and
stood looking expectantly on.   I judged from her
manner, as she stood there, gazing at me with a
species of gloating triumph, that she quite expected
to see her husband throw me bodily into the street,
or thrash me within an inch of my life.   For either
of these results she was prepared; but for the result
which actually followed I cannot think she was quite
so well prepared.   Hanna, too, was entirely convinced that he could heap all manner of insults upon
me, or strike or kick me with the greatest impunity,
and he determined to use his power to the utmost.

"Now, sir," he said to me in a loud and insulting
tone, "take your stuff and get out of here."

Having thus spoken, he waited for me to obey his
insulting behest, but his manner showed that he had
some doubts as to whether I would do so or not.
For my part I realized the utter uselessness of attempting to reason further with him, and I determined to
set my valises behind the office counter, and ask that

they might be allowed to remain there until the morrow, or until such time as I could find another lodging-place. With this purpose in view I left my chair and advanced to take up the valises. I was hardly conscious at the time—though I have thought of it since—of the look of exultation that leaped into Hanna's eyes as I advanced. He thought (I know now) that, craven, like, I intended to take my baggage and slink away, and he probably thereupon determined to give me something to remember him by.

As I bent slowly and with difficulty over, for my body was stiff from long illness, Hanna gave me a violent kick from behind. This cowardly and unprovoked assault was so violent, as well as unexpected, that I was taken wholly by surprise, and fell heavily forward upon my face. The kick and the fall together caused me very severe pain, and, indeed, came near crippling me. I soon scrambled to my feet, and my anger was past all control. I forgot my age, my weakness, my diseased frame. All the vigor of early manhood returned in that moment—every fibre within me quivered and shook with a mighty indignation.

Hanna, not dreaming that I would return his blow after the usual Texas fashion—with interest and upon the spot, stood near at hand, flushed and triumphant.

"Hanna," said I, "I will break every bone in your craven body for this!" and he stepped hastily back, with his hands thrown out, and with an expression of sickly terror upon his face. Without more ado, I rushed upon him and struck him with such fury

and address that I felled him to the floor at the first
blow. My Irish friend, who had looked on in silence
up to this time, now sprang excitedly from his chair
and cried out:

"Give 'im h—, Nall; give 'im h—!"

Mrs. Hanna ran across the room, sprang upon a
chair and screamed lustily. But my appetite for
revenge had not been appeased, and I meant to take
ample and speedy vengeance. Mounting, therefore,
upon the writhing body of my foe ere he could struggle to a sitting posture, I proceeded to punish him
severely. The Irishman danced about the room in
a high state of excitement, and called out encouragingly to me from time to time. But it chanced that
very little encouragement was needed to make me
pummell my foe severely. He yelled manfully, and
his wife, no doubt believing him to be in his last gasp,
ran shrieking from the house, calling "Police!" at
the top of her shrill voice at every leap. Hanna
howled louder than she, and between them, they
raised such a concert of hideous sounds as seldom
falls to mortal lot to hear. Hanna soon left off his
mad shrieks of terror and roared lustily for mercy.
By this time a crowd was rapidly collecting and, I
saw that the whole house would soon be filled with
them, hence I released my noisy foe and permitted
him to get up. I then sat down near the Irishman.
As soon as Hanna once more found himself master
of his own movements, he struggled hastily to his
feet and ran behind the counter. As he now appeared, no one, save a Stoic, could behold him with-

out smiling. His back was covered wth the dust of the floor on which he had wallowed, his face was red and swollen, his fair frowzed, his collar awry, his necktie torn partly off, and his vest and shirt were both rent. He made no effort to come out from behind his counter, but remained there until a policeman came, glowering at me from time to time with an expression of mingled hate, malice and fear—a look which I returned, though neither of us said a word. Indeed, as our blood—speaking for myself at least—had been heated by the contest, and the characteristic Anglo-American fighting instinct thoroughly aroused, one word would have brought about a renewal of the struggle.

My enthusiastic Irish friend was congratulating me upon my victory, when a policeman entered, followed by Mrs. Hanna. Her face was flushed, her hair disheveled, and she bore visible marks of perturbation and excitement. She gazed at me fearfully, and did not come anywhere near me. Hanna started joyfully when his restless eye fell upon the blue-coated form of the policeman, and his eye lighted up with vindictive pleasure. It was some moments, however, before he ventured to come from behind his counter, and then only when the officer had come well within the room.

"Which is the man?" said the policeman, pausing and looking about the office.

Mrs. Hanna pointed to me.

"That is the man, she said.

The officer advanced and placed his hand upon my arm.

You'll have to come with me," he said.

"Very well, I am ready. But are you going to arrest me and no one else?"

"Certainly I shall not arrest anyone else. You raised the row and did the fighting, and now you want me to arrest some one else."

I said no more, knowing that Mrs. Hanna had pejudiced the officer against me by her account of the affair, but went out into the street with him.

My landlady followed at a safe distance, calling out to the officer when she reached the street and advising him to lock me at once in a strong dark dungeon at the very least. She then went on to tell him in a shrill, high-pitched voice, that she and her husband would "be around" in the morning to testify against me and "have me hung;" that I had murdered her dear husband and she would have me sent up for life.

To this the official made no reply. Whether he was speculating as to the means by which Mrs. Hanna could accomplish such a feat in jurisprudence as to first "hang me," and afterwards "send me up for life," does not appear. But I think that the vindictive and malevolent spirit she showed upon this occasion was one of the indirect causes of turning the scale of the officer's sympathy from their side to mine. At any rate his manner toward me began to change somewhat, and he questioned me, asking me how I came to involve myself in such trouble, etc.

In reply I gave him a full account of the events that had befallen me since my arrival in the city; of

the nature of the understanding between Mrs. Hanna
and myself; of the smooth stranger who had indirectly
involved me in my present trouble;—and, in short,
of everything that had happened to me since the beginning of my sojourn in San Antonio.   He listened
attentively, and at the conclusion of my story, he
slapped me heartily upon the shoulder and said:

"My. friend, you have done exactly right, and while
I can't afford to encourage fighting, I must say that
if I had been in your place I should have thrashed
Hanna sooner than you did."

By this time we had reached the Recorder's office.
As we entered the policeman whispered to me:

"Tell him the same story you have told me, and,
my word for it, you will have nothing to fear."

Evidently, thought I, here is one partisan, at least;
and I walked up the room with a more confident step,
The Recorder was alone.   He glanced up as we
entered and said:

"What now?"

The policeman replied; giving a brief account of the
occurrences at the Cleveland House, and in a manner
which showed my side of the story in a very favora-
ble light.   I could see from the superior officer's
manner that he was already impressed in my favor.
He listened with attention, and when the policeman
had concluded, he asked me what I had to say for
myself.   In reply I defended myself as warmly and
as eloquently as I could, even relating certain parts of
my history previous to my arrival in San Antonio;
and when I had done, I thought that even a less in-

terested observer than myself could have detected a suspicious moisture in the Recorder's eyes.

He spoke to me very kindly, asked a few questions at points where my story had not been clear to him, and said he supposed he would have to excuse me, and I might go. It would not be easy to describe the exultation and almost boyish joy which possessed me on hearing this. Visions of narrow cells, and balls-and-chains, and a daily fare of bread and water, had been floating confusedly through my mind for an hour or more; and when these gloomy ideas, together with all prospect of punishment, were thus suddenly dispelled, my joy was great I thanked the Recorder in the warmest terms, and having received his kindest wishes for my future welfare, uttered with evident sincerity, I took leave of him and went out upon the street. I then started to return to the Cleveland · House, but had not gone more than two blocks when I heard some one loudly calling my name. I turned at once, and my heart sank within me when I beheld my friend the policeman running after me in a high state of excitement, waving his arms, and shouting my name in stentorian tones. I immediately concluded that the Recorder had changed his mind, or repented of his unusual kindness to me and had sent the officer to arrest me again. The sudden transition from the pleasant and even joyful train of thought that had occupied me, to what seemed now to be a clear prospect of imprisonment, was no less shocking than disheartening; and for cne brief instant I thought of attempting to evade the coming officer by flight.

Happily, however, I made no such attempt; but, restraining the impulse by a strong effort I calmly waited for the policeman to come up with me. In a few moments he came up panting.

"Here, Mr. Nall," said he, "give me your hand. I have got something for you."

I hesitated a moment, but not knowing what else to do, I complied with his request by holding out my hand to him. He seized it with his left, and with his right placed a bright silver dollar in my palm.

"There—there," he said, hastily, as he saw that I was about to speak, "not a word—I do not wish to hear a single word!" and he turned hurriedly about and ran back faster than he came. I called after him, and he waved his hand, but did not stop. I have never seen him since, and do not to this day know to whom I am indebted for that dollar. I stood gazing after his retreating form until it was lost in the distance, and then at the dollar. Finally, however, I placed it in my pocket in a very puzzled manner, and went on down the street. The money, little as it was, was indeed a God-send, for I did not have a cent in my pocket. I believed at the time— and I have seen no reason since for changing my opinion—that the kind-hearted Recorder, whose sympathy I had touched, and whose name I do not know to this day, had sent me the money.

I now knew that I could count upon at least two friends in the city, and this knowledge comforted me greatly. With a lighter heart I pursued my way to the Cleveland House. When I entered the office

no one was present but my Irish friend "Jim."
"Well," said he, looking up with a smile as I sat
down, "it seems they didn't lock you up in the
'cooler' after all."

"No," I returned, "the Recorder 'excused' me, and
here I am."

"I'm glad of that," said my friend.

A chambermaid passed through the office at that
moment, and I showed her my piece of money and
said to her:

"You may tell your mistress that I shall remain
here until to-morrow. I have the money, as you see,
and this is a public house."

A few minutes after this supper was announced,
and when this meal was over, I took my valises from
the office, and carried them up to Irish Jim's rooms.
At his request I remained with him all night. There
was an extra couch in his bed-chamber, and I occupied it. We locked our door securely, and so prepared ourselves that we might not be taken off our
guard in case Hanna should make any attack upon
me. I did not anticipate anything of the kind, but
we thought it best to be prepared. It was my intention to leave San Antonio on the following morning en route for Wooten Wells. These wells possess
great medicinal virtues, and Dr. Herf had advised
me to go there if I could We were not disturbed
during the night except by dreams, and after breakfast the next morning my friend Jim gave me a letter
to the conductor of one of the passenger trains on
which I could travel the greater part of the distance

to Wooten Wells and thus save the price of a ticket.
This was the more necessary, as I did not have it,
my sole possessions in cash being limited to the sum
of one dollar.   For obvious reasons I shall not mention the name of the conductor, nor of the railway.
When the long train, loaded with passengers, came
puffing up to the depot and stopped, and its living
freight began to alight, I boarded it, and went into
the car just back of the "smoker."

Shortly after the train steamed out of the station
the conductor began his rounds.   When he came to
me I handed him the letter given me by Jim.   The
official read it without comment; and handing it back
to me when he had done so—

"I cannot take you, my friend," he said.   "You
will have to pay your fare or get off."   And he held
out his hand for the money I did not have.

I gazed at him for some moments in silence, and I
then asked him if he had a pistol.   He replied that
he had not; and, looking at me strangely, desired
to know what I wanted with a pistol.

"I want to kill myself," I replied, in tragically
sepulchral tones.

The conductor stared at me with bulging eyes for
a moment, the very picture of astonishment and
trepidation, and then went hurriedly on, and he did
not approach me again.   No doubt he felt he had
fallen in with a dangerous lunatic, and that he would
be particularly fortunate if he escaped with his life.
At any rate he was careful to avoid me, and whenever his eye fell upon me his sunburned skin turned

to a swarthy pallor. The fare amounted to several dollars, I do not remember how many.

When we reached Hearne later in the day we changed cars for Wooten Wells. At this place I bought a ticket for the latter town, at the cost, I think, of fifty-five cents, leaving me forty-five cents, and this was all I had. The reader will remember that this dollar was given me by the Recorder, otherwise I should have been entirely destitute of money, and would have been under the disagreeable necessity of either remaining in San Antonio, or of walking to my destination. That small piece of money had been worth more to me at the time than ever dollar was before. We steamed into Wooten Wells sometime after midnight, and I was the only passenger to alight. The sky had become overcast, and an obscuring mist hung over the earth. Now and then some rain had fallen. The long train rumbled on its way, its red lights gleaming like fiery eyes through the mist. The darkness was intense, and enough rain had fallen to make the roads muddy and disagreeable. There was no one in or about the depot but the station agent and a porter. No omnibus, coach, carriage, or vehicle of any kind, and the only means the traveler had of reaching any of the hotels were such as he had brought with him;—namely, his feet.

The porter informed me that it was a full mile to the nearest hotel—the Jackson House, and he further added that only an ordinary boggy country road led to it. I therefore had no recourse but to take my

valises and set off down the dark muddy roadway.
This I did, slipping and floundering about in the
darkness and mud, while now and then gusts of wind
and light showers of rain passed over me. I thought
that mile the longest I had ever traveled, and feared
it would never end; but finally, tired—indeed, almost
exhausted (for I had no strength), wet, footsore,
covered with mud, and hungry and sleepy, I reached
the Jackson House.

CHAPTER IX.

I AM TOLD OF MY OWN DEATH.

i'

True religion
Is alwaya mild, propitious and humble;
Plays not the tyrant, plants no faith in blood
Nor bears destruction on her chariot wheels.
                                        —*Miller*.

Wooten Wells, though widely known as a valetu-
dinarian resort, could hardly be called a town.
There was one small store devoted to general mer-
chandise, and a few private residences scattered
about. The principal hostelries were the Jackson
House and the Roan Hotel. Messrs. Roan and
Jackson were equal partners, and each was manager
of the house which bore his name. Thus, although
Mr. Jackson was manager of the Jackson House, he
was but part proprietor, the other half being owned
by Mr. Roan, and vice versa.

These two men, thus associated in the management
of the principal industry of the place, were in their
mental make-up as wide apart as the poles. Indeed,
I doubt whether, in the course of a number of years
spent in the study of human character, I have ever
seen two natures which seemed to have so little in
common. But their different traits will be more fully
revealed as our narrative advances.

After breakfast on the morning of my arrival, I sought out Mr. Jackson, who was a kind-hearted gentleman, and told him that I had come to his town for the benefit of my health, which had long been in a critical condition—indeed, that an eminent physician had given me up to die and—I asked him to give me such employment about his place as I could do to pay for my board and lodging. In reply, he spoke in the kind manner that was natural to him, and told me that I might remain, as he thought suitable employment for me would not be hard to find; that he would give the matter a night's reflection and let me know his decision on the morrow. With this promise the interview ended.

On the night of my arrival I had slept on the ground floor in a small apartment near the office, and somewhere about sunrise had been awakened by the sound of voices. On account of the intervening wall I could hear, but not see, the voices of several gentlemen in conversation in the office, and in the tones of one of them I recognized the voice of an old gentleman whom I had known for many years in my old home. His name was Payne, but he was more familiarly known as Judge Payne from having served as judge of Hopkins County. I knew that he was familiar with my history, and would recognize me at sight. This was a contingency which I had not calculated upon, and which I now determined to avoid. The reader will easily guess that my desire to hear late news from my family, and from my old home, was very strong, and I wondered if there were

any means by which I could learn such intelligence
from Judge Payne without betraying myself. At
least I determined to do so, if it were possible, by
any strategem which I could devise. On leaving Mr.
Jackson that morning I hurried into the office, and,
to make assurance doubly sure, examined the regis-
ter. After some trouble I found the name, "Judge
Payne, Sulphur Springs, Texas." By a few cautious
inquiries I learned that the Judge had been stopping
at Wooten Wells for a week or more, and that he
would probably return home on the next day. I
therefore made two resolves; namely, that I must be
careful to avoid a meeting with him on that day; and,
second, that I must question him, if I did so at all,
without delay. The first was comparatively an easy
matter; the second difficult if not impossible. Chance,
however, favored me, and threw the desired opportunity in my way.

After supper that evening several gentlemen collected, in true lawyer fashion, around the heater in
the office, and engaged in conversation. Among the
party was Judge Payne. The small apartment was
but dimly and partially lighted by an oil lamp which
depended from the ceiling. The Judge sat with his
back to a door which was thrown open. Now, back
of this door when it was thus wide open was a small
recess in the wall where faces were washed and heads
combed. There were mirrors, wash-basins, brushes
and such paraphernalia; and anyone engaged in
brushing his hair or washing his face was entirely
concealed, or nearly so, by the door when it swung

back.   I was in this alcove performing my ablutions
when the group of gentlemen mentioned entered the
room and took seats about the heater.   As soon as
I perceived that Judge Payne was among them, I
inwardly rejoiced, for I saw that chance had given
me the opportunity so greatly desired. And I resolved
to make the best of it.   The conversation had lulled
(this may seem to be an extraordinary circumstance,
as these gentlemen were all lawyers; yet we repeat,
that the conversation had lulled) and at this moment
one of the gentlemen asked:

"What is the character, Judge—the main natural
features,   I   might   say,—of   the   country   in   your
county?"

I mentally thanked the gentleman for this question,
as it opened an easy way for me to ask several inquiries that were trembling upon my tongue.   The
Judge, pleased at so good an opportunity to pay a
glowing tribute to his native county, answered at
some length.   When he had finished, I spoke, rubbing my hands noisily in the water:

"Are you acquainted, Judge, may I ask, with many
people in the county seat of Hopkins County?"

"Oh, yes!" he replied, supposing me to be merely
a curious stranger, "I   know   a   great   many   people
there."

"Some years ago," said I, "I   went   through   that
section of country, and stopped there for quite a
while.   I got acquainted with a number of persons.
There was one in particular whom I have never heard
from since that I should like to inquire about, but I

cannot think of his name. He lived in a large white house on a hill north of the town, and did business, I think, on the public square. I cannot recall his name, but it seems to me it begins with an 'F.'"

"Oh yes," said the obliging Judge, "perhaps you are thinking of Fleming—E. B. Fleming?"

"Yes," said I, agitating the water with both hands, "that is the name. Do you happen to know where he is at present?"

"Yes," he rejoined; "Fleming is dead, poor fellow. He became broken up in business, lost his property and, went insane. He was taken to an asylum, and stayed there a number of years—I don't remember how many."

"But I believe you said he was dead?"

"Yes, I was going to add that he finally made his escape from the asylum, wandered away, and was drowned. A sad affair. Fleming was a good citizen, and an enterprising man. He met with a terrible fate."

Then there was silence for some moments, and I continued my questioning of the innocent old Judge. I asked him a great many questions, and received answers which, if set down here, would probably only weary the reader. The information so greatly desired was learned from him so far as he could give it to me. Finally, however, either wondering at the great length of time I required to perform my ablutions, or else having some desire to see the man who had shown such unusual curiosity about a strange town, the Judge moved his chair slightly beyond the door, and turned and looked at me. But I saw the movement in time, and hastily buried my face in the large towel, and was so long about drying it that he turned again to the crowd in front of him. Fearing that I had aroused his suspicions, or awakened his curiosity, which amounted to the same thing, I immediately escaped through the door and left the house. On the following day he returned to his home in Sulphur Springs, and that was the last time I ever saw him. The questions that I had asked him had not, as I had feared, aroused his suspicions. Open as the day himself, he was the last man to harbor suspicions towards, or be distrustful of, anyone. A few months after his return home, the last messenger came for him, and he died in the full belief that I had passed on ahead of him.

I remained at Wooten Wells for several months, and only left it for reasons which shall be made known. The work assigned me by my kind friend Mr. Jackson, was in his flower-yard and subsequently in his garden. The employment was light and easily done, and had the emoluments been great enough I should have had a sinecure. Indeed, the labor was beneficial rather than otherwise, and did me a great deal of good in thus supplying light employment for both body and mind. Roan came over to the Jackson House pretty often, and his presence was never desired by anyone. Short, stubby, and selfish, as well as domineering, he was liked by very few.

He came to me one day and contumeliously ordered me to take my meals thereafter at the servant's table.

Now, the servants were principally negroes, and a
command to sit at the servant's table was equivalent
to being ordered to dine with negroes.

"What do you mean, sir?" I demanded, in a rage.

"I mean, sir, he yelled, his squat figure puffing
and swelling like Æsop's frog, and his round bulging
eyes glaring prodigiously from his fat red face, "I
mean, sir, for you to take your proper place. We
don't feed servants like gentlemen, I'd have you
know! And furthermore, sir, I'd have you know that
you are talking to *me!*" and he swelled and puffed
and fumed and got redder and rounder an more frog-
like every moment.

"Well sir," I returned, "your commands are wasted
upon me. I shall continue as I have begun, all the
brutes in Wooten Wells to the contrary notwithstanding." And with that I turned about and left
him, staring after me in wonder, wrath, and astonishment, and working himself up into a mighty rage.

I paid no further attention to him; but some days
after I was doing some light work in the garden when
Roan came up; and, affecting to be oblivious of my
presence, began examining some work done by a
negro. Several rows of English peas in one corner
were the objects of his attention. He stood looking
upon them as if he expected the whole row to fall
down in mute homage before him. The negro had
thrust some sticks down into the ground beside each
vine for them to grow upon, and Roan was not
pleased with the work. Indeed, after staring at them
for a time, he became enraged, and seizing a hoe

began to cut them down, sticks and all, root and branch, cursing volubly with each stroke of the hoe.

I stood and watched him in silence for several minutes. Obviously, the man who could thus destroy property, either his own or some one else's, in a fit of captious rage, needed restraining. I asked him what he was doing. As he made no reply—

"Roan," said I, disgusted at his mighty rage over so small a matter, "you are a fool."

At this he paused, his round red face, streaming with perspiration, and heated by the vigor of his efforts, growing suddenly rounder redder and hotter, and glaring at me, he yelled:

"Do you know whom you are talking to?"

"Well sir," I rejoined, "I think I do. I am talking to a captious fool."

"What!" he fumed, violently, "you—you—y-y-ou —can leave! You can get out from here, and stay out, sir!"

"Certainly I can," I retorted. "And I can say to you that you are the worst brute in this country. You great puffed, moon-faced, unappreciative, domineering, coarse imbecile!"

He raged dreadfully at this, and from his antics, his prodigious puffing, and his squat figure heaving and swelling, I thought he would burst. One would have thought, not unnaturally, from such conduct as this that the man had gone stark mad. He did not, however, make any attack upon me. I determined to fire one more shot at him; for (let me confess) I was considerably enraged, and too angry to be considerate or to choose my words.

"I have been wanting to leave here for some time,"
I said to him, when he had calmed down sufficiently
for my words to be heard, "because I have not been
in the habit of associating with brutes. I have seen
villains and scoundrels before, but you are the greatest
of all that I have yet seen." After waiting a moment
for his reply, which was not forthcoming, I turned
and left him.

It was then morning, and I determined to leave
Wooten Wells that afternoon. A small town known
by the name of Bremond was only three miles away;
and as there was no railroad connection between
the two places, I resolved to make the journey on
foot. My friend Jackson was sorry that any "misun-
derstanding" as he termed it, had occurred, and sorry
that Roan and myself had disagreed. His deprecation
of the affair, however sincere, did not mend matters;
and had I been given the alternative of leaving immediately, or apologizing to Roan, I should unhesitatingly have chosen the former. I did not in the
least regret what I had said to him, and did not care
whether he relished it or not. In truth, I do not
think it would have been safe for him to have approached me for any purpose, friendly or otherwise.

Accordingly, I set out about the middle of the
afternoon on my journey to Bremond. I walked
along leisurely in the mild spring air, and reflected
upon the incidents of my stay at Wooten Wells. I
had not, fortunately for myself, fallen a victim to
any of the advertising "doctors" who abounded there,
although others had; and if I had received no benefit,

I at least had not been harmed.   There were at that
time—and may be yet—a swarm of advertising
"doctors" and other quacks and social cormorants,
who haunted the hotels, and fastened their talons
upon every "patient" who came in their way, and
lucky was he who escaped them.

I had not walked more than half of the league
which lay between the two villages, when I perceived
a gentleman approaching me in a one-horse vehicle.
In a short time we met, and I saw before me a man
in the meridian of life, with a countenance striking
and remarkable for its expression of open and friendly
benevolence.   I thereupon stopped him and we entered into conversation.   He had not spoken half a
dozen words before I saw that he was a minister,
and his appearance certainly comported in every
visible respect with his calling.

"I should say, friend," said he, "that you are a
stranger in these parts."

"I am, sir," returned I.   And I proceeded to give
him an account of my stay at Wooten Wells, and
such other facts as I thought proper to tell him.

"And how am I to call your name?" he asked,
looking at me out of the corners of his eyes.

"Nall," I answered, "R. M. Nall."

"And mine," said he, "is J. H. Rowland.   I am
the pastor of the Baptist church at Bremond.   And
you are looking for some place to stop—some place
where you can get light employment and board?"

I answered in the affirmative.   He bent his head,
as if in meditation, for some moments, fingering his

beard abstractedly, and tapping his toe against the
wheel of his vehicle.

"Well, Mr. Nall," said he at length, raising his
head to look at me with a very meditative expression
of countenance, "we (meaning himself) are not very
rich, and our house, which is our own, is not very
commodious, but our hearts are willing; and if you
think you can put up with our poor accomodations,
you may remain with us for a time. May be as we
grow better acquainted we can hit upon some arrangement that will please all around. My wife is at home,
with her children. We have two grown daughters
and some smaller boys and girls. Do you think this
would suit you?"

I told him gratefully and even eagerly that it
would. His manner was markedly kind and friendly,
and very winning. He then gave me minute directions as to route, how to find his house, etc., and what
to do when I got there. He then reached me his
hand, shook mine warmly and, drove on, but called
back after he had gone a short distance to say that
he himself would return later on that afternoon. I
could not forbear congratulating myself upon this
meeting and its results, and walked on in a better
frame of mind.

In the course of half an hour I reached the home of
the kind-hearted minister. It was a large white frame
dwelling, situated in the outskirts of the village. I
knocked at the door, and had no sooner made known
the object of my visit than I was invited to enter and
the family treated me with great friendliness and

cordiality. The ladies were modest, pure-minded and innocent, and knew little of the great world beyond them. I endeavored to entertain them with accounts of my experiences in the various States of the Union that I had visited, until parson Rowland returned, some hours later that afternoon.

I remained with this family for some weeks. Each afternoon I went to the village postoffice for the minister's mail. The office was situated considerably more than a mile from the Rev. Rowland's, and for some reason was located on an obscure side street, or road, which was always silent and deserted. One afternoon some weeks after my arrival, having as usual gone to the postoffice, which the postmaster kept in the extreme back end of a building near two hundred feet in length, and secured the mail, I observed, on emerging from the building, a one-armed man standing on the sidewalk. At that moment a carriage, containing a man and a woman, drove up to the pavement and came to a halt. As they approached I happened to glance at the one-armed man —whom we will call Smith—and I saw that he was gazing at the couple with an expression not good to see. The moment the vehicle came to a stop, the gentleman started to spring out upon the pavement; but ere he could do so the one-armed man came silently but swiftly forward and confronted him. The gentleman in the carriage turned pale and sank back into his seat. The lady beside him, who, as I afterwards learned, was his wife, was small and determined-looking, and *she* did not grow pale as Smith

stood before them with clenched hand and flushed·
face. No, obviously, if appearances went for anything, she was a brave and daring little woman, and
possessed of that dauntless courage which ladies
ordinarily do *not* possess. The sequel will show that
her appearance did not belie her character.

No one was in sight. No object, great or small,
moved upon the street, and we four were alone. I
waited in the doorway to learn the issue of the scene.

"Worth," began one-armed Mr. Smith, in tones
husky and tremulous with rage, "you are an infernal
villain! I have long wanted an opportunity to tell
you so."

Worth* was a large man, with an excellent
physique, and in full possession of all means of offense
or defense with which nature had endowed him. He
was large enough and strong enough, had he been
brave enough, to have easily conquered his smaller
adversary in single combat, even had the latter gentleman possessed two arms instead of one. But the
stout, strong-limbed man, with a capacity for great
and sustained physical exertion, only cowered before
his physically insignificant opponent, turned pale and
red by turns, and finally stammered out that he "did
not want any trouble."

"Trouble," said his enemy, in angry scorn; "no
you dirty villain; but you are quite ready to make it
with your base lying tongue—ready to blacken the
characters of helpless women, and to forever blight

---

* These name are pseudonyms. The true names are not given for
obvious reasons.

the lives and prospects of innocent girls. You detestable heartless villain!"

Worth trembled, but made no reply. Smith gazed upon him for some moments in silence, and was evidently struggling with himself for his features worked convulsively, and he clenched and unclenched his hand in a manner too suggestive to be mistaken. Then, as if other thoughts had suddenly swept over him, the expression of his countenance changed in an instant from hesitating anger to furious and ungovernable rage, and he edged closer to the trembling coward in the vehicle and struck him several stinging blows. The big rascal only threw up his hands and crouched lower in his seat. As is usual in such cases, the more Smith gave way to his anger, the more furious he became; and so, from striking a few blows he began to shower them down upon Worth's head like rain. The latter took them in silence for a while, or only uttered low, terrified moans, but as they grew in force he began to whine and cry to Smith to "Quit—quit, I say! Quit now! Oh, you quit!" with much more to the same purpose.

Even then no one came in sight; and the only one who might have heard Worth's groans—the postmaster—was shut up in his office near two hundred feet away.

My attention up to this point had been bestowed entirely upon the two men, but now I glanced at Mrs. Worth. The expression upon her face struck me at once, and though she was silent and motionless, the dilated eyes, glittering and sparkling like

living coals, the swelling nostrils, the cheek now
ghastly white and now suffused with red; the com-
pressed lip and tightly-clenched hands;—all these
bespoke the volcano within.   She, it was obvious,
possessed the physical courage so markedly absent
in her unworthy consort.

While these thoughts were running through my
mind, she rose in her seat and sprang with the furv
and silent swiftness of a tigress upon their one-armed
foe.   Her frame was slight and delicate, but, surprised by the energy and celerity of her onset, Smith
staggered back a few steps, and she slipped to the
ground.   The next moment one of her slim hands
was buried in the long beard of her adversary, and
the other busy upon his face.   In an instant of time
several streams of blood were trickling down his
cheeks.   He endeavored to push her backward, or
to disengage himself, but she clung to him with a
tenacity that baffled all his efforts.   Yet she had not
uttered a word, or screamed or made the least outcry
as women commonly do at such moments.

I saw that Smith, unable to release himself, and
equally unable to strike a woman, even in his rage,
was becoming desperate, and must soon lose his self-
control.   In the latter case I shuddered to think
what might follow.   He struggled almost frantically
to release himself.   But she had his beard in a tight
grip, and he was comparatively helpless.   His face
was badly scratched and disfigured, and blood was
running freely from each wound made by the infuri-
ated woman.

At length he commanded her, in a hoarse and strident voice that might have warned her, to release him, but she clung to him all the tighter. He then repeated the command in a voice that made the trembling occupant of the vehicle start. This, like the first, was disregarded, and the frantic man demanded, for the third time, "Madam, turn me loose!"

He then waited a moment to ascertain whether she would obey, and as she gave no sign of doing so, he raised his foot—his only means of defense under the circumstances—and bestowed a powerful kick upon the enraged woman. The blow was so furious that she released her hold upon him and, staggered and fell. In a moment, however, she was upon her feet again, and endeavored to attack him. He kicked her a second time, and she fell in a heap in the center of the road, almost insensible. The maddened man rushed at her again, when, having recovered from the astonishment that had held me spell-bound and motionless, I hurried forward and grasped him by the arm.

"For God's sake, man," I cried, as I seized him with all my strength, "forbear! Would you strike a woman? You have killed her now!"

He turned pale at this and said:

"You are right, my friend, whoever you are. I think I must have been gone here," and he touched his head with a significant gesture.

The woman opened her eyes and rose unsteadily to her feet. Whispering to Smith that he had better go, which he instantly did, without stopping to thank me, and soon disappearing down the street, without pausing or stopping to look behind, I assisted the lady to return to her carriage. She was somewhat stunned from the force of the blows that had struck her to the ground, and apathetic from the reaction of feeling, but otherwise uninjured. As soon as she had resumed her seat, the carriage was driven rapidly away.

CHAPTER X.

As I walked towards home from the postoffice, I thought of all that I had heard concerning the Worth family. Mrs. Worth was older than her husband by a few years, and I had been told that she was a widow when she married Worth. They were comparatively wealthy, and the lady was esteemed as an energetic, business like woman, kind to her husband and to everyone else, and of a quiet unassuming disposition. Her husband on the contrary was accused of having a base mercenary turn, meddlesome, gossiping, idle, indolent, and very indulgent indeed to his own appetites and desires. Whether this was true or not, it was notorious that he was in constant trouble over something that he had said, or had threatened to say, and was freely accused of slandering everyone against whom he cherished enmity or dislike.

I had not yet reached the minister's when I heard the swift roll of wheels behind me, and the very couple of whom I was then thinking drove up, hailed me, and stopped.

"You are a stranger to us, sir," began Mrs. Worth, (she looked weak and ill, but spoke with considerable strength;) "but your conduct this afternoon (she flushed as she spoke this,) has convinced us that you are not a bad man, and that you can aid us."

I assured her that I was quite willing to do so if it lay within my power.

"Well," she proceeded, more firmly, "myself and Mr. Worth here," she indicated him by a wave of her hand, but did not look at him, "have been intending for some days past to go on a fishing excursion in a two-horse wagon overland. We want some reliable person to drive this wagon, loaded with our outfit, and leading a couple of animals behind, across the country to Marlin. We will follow later in our buggy. Can you do this for us?"

"When should you wish me to start?"

"To-morrow morning, as early as possible."

"Then I can go."

"Very well," she replied. "We thank you, and here is the money for your trouble." She handed me a bank-bill and drove off, after asking me to come to their house early on the morrow. As they disappeared around a distant corner I glanced at the bank-note, and observed, with no little astonishment, as well as pleasure, that it was ten dollars. I walked onward in high good humor, for I thought that perhaps I might yet accumulate sufficient money to purchase a ticket to California. Dr. Herf had told me that so long as I had diabetes, I might live for years in the mild and salubrious climate of the Pacific coast, while my span of life could not last long in any climate less mild. In short, a sojourn in California meant life to me, while a stay in Texas meant death. It had therefore been my chief aim for the past few months to acquire means to make my way to the Pacific coast, and every cent I obtained was treasured and hoarded to this end.

I went on home immediately, and put the money into the hands of the Rev. Mr. Rowland. I informed him of the conversation between Mrs. Worth and myself, and he advised me by all means to go, as he could see no objection to my doing so. Promptly, therefore, the next morning I presented myself at the home of the Worth's, and was met at the door by the lady herself.

"Ah! Mr. Nall," said she, with a smile of satisfaction, "you have come. Walk in, sir, until we are ready for you."

But as we were entering the parlor Mr. Worth came striding through the hall to say that the wagon was prepared for me. He then led the way into the back yard, where the vehicle stood. I went up and examined it curiously. The bed of the wagon had a substantial covering of white duck stretched over a frame, and a large mare, not in the best condition, with a young colt standing by her side, was hitched to the back end of the running-gear. On the inside of the wagon were a number of articles—cooking utensils, cooking materials, and other things that a couple of well-to-do young people might carry with them on a six weeks' jaunt about the country.

"Now what we want you to do, Mr. Nall," said the lady, who had followed us into the yard, and who

seemed to be the real business man of the establishment, "is to drive this wagon and team, and the mare
and colt behind it, to Marlin and, deliver them to
Mr. Jones, proprietor of the Jones Hotel. The mare
may not be very easy to lead, but by all means take
her there. Say to Mr. Jones that we shall follow in
our buggy, in case you reach there ahead of us. We
shall more than likely get to Marlin as soon as, or
before, you do; but if we do not, please wait for us."

While she was speaking Mr. Worth had opened a
large gate near at hand and driven the team outside.
I waited a moment to receive a few additional instructions, and then, mounting the driver's seat, I
drove off down the road. Recent and copious rains
had swollen all the streams in that section and,
indeed, had made brooks, creeks and rivulets where
none had been for years. My road led me over the
left fork of the Brazos and other streams. The
thoroughfares were muddy, slippery, and really unfit
for travel.

The mare came along behind the wagon with very
good grace for a time, but finally she became obstinate, and worried me exceedingly. I determined
however, to be delayed no longer than was necessary
by the blind contumacy of an animal, and so when
the mare hung back, and did not follow fast enough,
thus causing the team in front to stop altogether at
times, I whipped them up vigorously. Upon this
they would make a desperate plunge forward, and
the obstinate mare was compelled to break into a
sullen unwilling trot.

After worrying along in this manner for some hours, the mare, on starting down a steep declivity, as usual, declined to advance further than the top, and in causing the team to lunge forward, the rope was broken. When this catastrophe occurred, the mare made no attempt to run away, but stood stiffly on the top of the ridge.

A farmhouse was fortunately near at hand, and taking two boxes of axle-grease from among the store in the wagon, I went to the gate and shouted "halloa!" A rope which would suit my purpose, and which was nearly new, hung on the fence. In answer to my cry a man came out of the house and approached the gate.

"My friend," I began, without any other preliminaries, "I am driving that team yonder, and am having some trouble with a horse I am leading—in fact, have just broken the only rope I had. This rope here on your fence would suit me. I have in my hand two boxes of good axle-grease which I will give you for the rope."

"Very well," said he, without betraying the least surprise, or emotion of any kind, "take the rope along and leave the axle-grease."

This I did, and having thanked him, hurried back and tied my new rope to the long wiry neck of the mare and fastened the other end to the wagon.

I then mounted the seat and drove off, the farmer watching me from his gate. The mare behaved very well for a time, as she had done at first, for she seemed to realize that I had secured a stouter rope.

But just as I had begun to delude myself with the hope that my trouble with the obstinate creature was over, she paused on the side of a slight declivity and refused to advance a step. I found myself under the necessity of stretching her lean neck to an extraordinary length before she consented to come along.

Matters went on in the uusal way for a number of miles until, almost without warning, the second rope snapped like a thread. Fortunately this occurred directly in front of a farmhouse standing on the roadside. The farmer himself was sitting on the piazza, and an immense chain, with huge steel links, known as a log-chain, was stretched at length on some hooks upon the wall. I resolved instantly to purchase the chain if possible, as I knew that whatever else it might do, it certainly would not break. Casting my eyes hastily over the contents of the wagon I selected a keg of molasses, and lifting it into view, addressed the man on the piazza and offered him the molasses for the chain.

"All right," said he, "I'll trade anything I've got. Bring the molasses here and get the chain."

This I did very eagerly, and I could not suppress the slight feeling of triumph which came over me as I fastened the chain around the neck of the mare and thence to the wagon. The gentleman on the piazza looked on curiously as I performed this task, and when it was done, he observed, sententiously:

"You have got her now."

"Why, I think I have, and it rejoices me to think so," I responded. "She has given me trouble enough."

With that I climbed up to the seat and drove off, looking back to see how the mare would behave under the circumstances. Very little urging was needed to make her trot on stiffly after the wagon, and I had no trouble with her for near half an hour. Then she became, or seemed to become, more obstinate than ever. We had a great many small pools of muddy water to cross and other bad spots in the road. At all such places she pulled back with all her might, but the contest between the lean and obstinate mare and a vigorous team under the lash, was short, and invariably resulted in a decisive victory for the team. I thought, however, more than once that we should infallibly pull her head off, but we did not; and the only visible result seemed to be that the offending head became very large and very much swollen. Towards the end of the journey she took to lying down in the middle of the road, and I always dragged her until she changed her mind and rose to her feet.

I reached Marlin awhile before dark, and the mare by that time presented such an extraordinary appearance that the people stared at her in wonder as I passed. Her head and neck were so greatly swollen that all semblance of their real shape was lost, and she was covered with mud and dirt from head to foot. When I drove up to the Jones House and called for the proprietor he came out immediately, and his eye falling upon the miserable object at the end of the wagon, he exclaimed:

"Great Gad, man, what is that?"

By way of reply I gave him a brief account of the day's incidents, and he laughed boisterously.

"I had fully determined," I added, "to bring her head even if I brought no more."

The Worths had not arrived. I turned the team over to Jones according to instructions, and stopped with him for the night, as I could not return to Bremond until the morrow.

On the following morning when I came down to breakfast, I ascertained that the Worths had not come yet, and as by train time they were still absent, I did not wait for them. I reached Bremond early in the afternoon. After supper that night someone called for me at the minister's gate, and on being invited to enter, refused to do so, at the same time requesting that I should come out to the gate.

On reaching the yard I found myself in the presence of Mr. Smith, the one-armed man. He greeted me very politely, and requested me to walk with him a short distance. When we had gone out of earshot of the house, and not before, he spoke:

"I suppose you know, Mr. Nall," said he, "that no one but yourself witnessed that little affair of yesterday?"

I told him that I did.

"Well," he resumed, "I have understood that you are in a low state of health, and are very anxious to get a new lease upon life by going to the Pacific coast. May I ask if that is not true?"

Wondering, I nevertheless assured him that it was.

"Now then," he continued, "if you are anxious to get off as soon as you can, and you can make it convenient to leave at once, please accept this money from me," and he placed five-and-twenty dollars in greenbacks in my hand.

"Hold a moment," said I, "and let me fully understand you. You do not want me to appear as a witness against you, and are willing to assist me as far on my way to California as this money will pay if I will leave at once?"

"Yes," returned he; "that is my desire."

"Very well, then," I responded, taking the money and placing it securely in my pocket, "I shall leave to-morrow."

With that he shook hands and parted.

I secured the ten dollars Mrs. Worth had given me from the good-hearted parson, and added it to my twenty-five. The next day I was speeding away as fast as steam could carry me. I had a brother, Mr. W. E. Fleming, residing in western Texas, and it was to him that I now went for an additional supply of money. He gave me what I asked for,* and I purchased a ticket for San Francisco, and in the beginning of summer began my long journey to the Pacific coast.

* It is but just to state that this was not the first time that Mr. W E. Fleming had given money to his brother, Mr. E. B. Fleming, during his illness.

CHAPTER XI.

Oh, it was pitiful!
Near a whole city full
Home she had none   —*Hood*.

We reached San Francisco in the summer of the year 1889, arriving in the city at night, and though my pockets were light—so light, indeed, that they contained nothing but a penknife—I went immediately to a respectable hotel. I remained here during the rest of the night, and got breakfast there the next morning. I then wandered out into the city, with the intention of finding some employment. But the day passed, and when night came I had found nothing. Anyone like myself, not bred to any trade or profession who has ever sought for employment in the streets of a strange city, well knows what a disheartening task it is. Indeed, I became discouraged more than once, but in spite of this, and the apparent futility of my quest, I persevered most earnestly. At many places where I applied, I met with cold rebuffs, or positive insults; at some, courteous treatment; and at all, refusal. But in the first case, when anyone offered me a positive insult, I contrived to make him speedily sensible that I would not sit quietly under unmerited affronts, and in the

215

next case, that politeness was never wasted upon me.

However, night closed, and the employment so earnestly sought had not been found. I had not so much as one cent in my pocket, and was wholly and entirely alone in the midst of a greater wilderness than any ever trodden by the children of Israel. I had gone without dinner, and I now realized the unwelcome fact that I must go without supper also. Nor was this the least of my troubles. I had no money to pay for the use of a bed, and would be under the disagreeable necessity of walking the streets all night. This was the only alternative, and I must own that it would cause me far greater suffering to walk from pavement to pavement in the damp air of night than would be occasioned by the loss of two meals. To add to my discomfort I had walked the streets during the whole day, and was not only footsore and weary, but with a frame weakened by disease, and unable to support me through times of cold, privation, or exposure, it will readily be seen that when night came I was ready to drop with fatigue. In this condition I was compelled to go out into the night, in the damp air and falling dew, with no covering but the star-strewn canopy of heaven, and wander to and fro the whole night through.

That was a dark hour for me, and for others as well; and I saw more than one wistful face, pallid and drawn with hunger, gazing longingly into the hundreds of brilliant shop windows laden with dainties, but none of whom, like the luckless Jean Valjean, ventured to take by force that which they could not acquire by purchase. During that dreadful night, of which I can never think without a shudder, I crept wearily from street to street from alley to alley, from square to square, and I thought the night would never end. Many unfortunates like myself roamed over the streets, but I could not have that sympathy for them that I have felt since. The pangs of hunger are harder to bear than almost any other earthly affliction, and I experienced only a feeling of rebellion against my fate and against the world. The calls of unappeased hunger, which no excuse can satisfy, and no artifice deceive, will lower us to the level of beasts of prey, as all the world knows.

I do not know how I lived through that night, nor how it passed, but finally, after a length of time which seemed interminable, day broke in the east. When morning came it seemed to me that long years had gone by since the day before. Ragged newsboys were soon hurrying over the streets, with batches of morning papers under their arms, and this suggested that possibly I might find something of interest in the "want" columns. An opportunity to glance over the *Examiner* soon presented itself, and I searched the "want" columns with some eagerness. In glancing down the sheet, scanning "wants" of almost every description, my eyes fell upon the following:

"Wanted—A few energetic men for light employment. Salary to begin on, $16 per week. No capital required. For particulars, apply at nine o'clock this A. M. at no. — Market-street."

The sentence, "No capital required," seemed to

suit the depleted condition of my purse, and I resolved
to apply. But the appointed time had not yet arrived,
and I had nearly two hours to wait. How I passed
the time I hardly know, but promptly on the stroke
of nine I ascended the stairway on Market street as
directed. I found that there were no less than forty
men there before me, and we all, needy adventurers
that we were, looked askance at one another, as if
each expected the other to deprive him of a sinecure.
It was a motely crowd, some among them being the,
worst specimens of humanity it had ever been my
lot to see.

We all stood, ranged according to our time of
arrival, before a door, mysteriously closed, which
only opened at irregular intervals to swallow one
of our number, like a hungry dragon. To carry the
simile further, none of those who were admitted ever
came out again, or at least if they did, we did not see
them. As so many were ahead of me, I had to wait
a full hour and, I did not dare to move from my
place, lest some one should assume it, as a number
had arrived after me. As only one was admitted at
a time, it was slow work; but finally, when my
patience was about exhausted, and I was ready to
drop to the floor through sheer fatigue, my turn came,
and I entered the mysterious portal. The room was
furnished in a very scanty manner, only a chair or
two, and a commodious desk, being visible. A gentleman was seated at the desk, writing in a big book.
He looked up as I entered and received me very
politely.

I soon learned the nature of the business. Mr. Underhill, this being the advertiser's name, was general agent for P. F. Collier, publisher, of New York. This firm, one of the largest in the world, had lately put an illustrated weekly in the field, with the apt name of *Once a Week*. Each subscriber to this journal received a number of handsome presents, and paid for the whole upon the instalment plan. The subscription price was about five dollars per year, and of this the canvassing agent got, as commission, nearly a dollar.

Mr. Underhill offered to furnish me with an outfit to canvass with, without exacting a deposit from me, and during the previous hour had put out some half a dozen canvassers. I had never done any work of the kind, but the bait was very tempting, and starvation stared me in the face. I therefore took the outfit and hurried away to take as many orders as I could, and in the shortest possible time. Yet I was weak and ill, and really unfit for work, almost tottering at times as I walked. One who has never canvassed for books in a large city cannot remotely imagine what disagreeable labor it is; but, sustained by the hope of earning a dollar with which to provide some of those physical comforts (necessities) which I had never properly valued until now, I went earnestly to work. That day's canvassing over the streets of San Francisco was far harder than ever was labor before to my weakened frame and diminished energies. Nothing, indeed, but the mere force of will-power prevented me from falling exhausted upon the street; but I bore up, knowing that the goal was near and the reward sweet.

Often during the day I was under the necessity of taking insults (which came principally from ladies) without so much as a murmur in reply, and all manner of rebuffs. I was very careful to give offense to none, and to conduct myself with as much dignity, politeness, and courtesy as was possible under the circumstances. As a result I was better treated, as I afterwards learned, than are most book-canvassers in San Francisco, and other large cities, although some rude treatment I could not and did not escape.

On account of physical exhaustion I was compelled to bring my day's work to a close some hours before sunset. I was very well satisfied, however, with what I had done, as I had taken a sufficient number of orders to net me $2.80, and strange to say I felt somewhat better as well as more hopeful. About the middle of the afternoon I returned the outfit to Mr. Underhill, and borrowed a dollar from him. He and I were conversing for a moment after he had handed me the money when a woe-begone and dejected figure darkened the doorway for a moment and advanced towards the desk. I recognized him as one of the men whom I had observed coming up the stairway after me that morning. He had a scratch on his face, his shoes and clothes were covered with dust, and he was a forlorn figure generally, while in his countenance disgust, dejection, anger, discouragement and cynicism were comically blended. He advanced silently and with lagging step, and laid his canvassing outfit upon the desk without a word.

"Well, what now?" demanded Mr. Underhill, too well bred to laugh at the man's lugubrious countenance, and yet inwardly convulsed.

"What now?" echoed the man, in a hollow voice, yet with infinite scorn, "you can take your d—d outfit. I don't want it."

"Why what's the matter?   Haven't you taken any orders?"

"No!" roared the man, in a sudden burst of rage. "Who the devil could?   I've been kicked down one stairway, thrust out of two houses, had my face slapped once, and hot water poured down my back. No more peddling for me.   I've simply discovered that I'm no book-agent."

Having thus spoken, he turned and limped away without another word, and soon disappeared down the stairs.

When the man was out of earshot, Mr. Underhill lay back in his chair and laughed until the tears rolled down his cheeks.

"Such scenes are of common occurrence, I suppose," I said, when he had left off, and was wiping his eyes.

"Yes indeed," he replied, wiping the last tear away and restoring his handkerchief to his pocket. "Only the fewest possible number of men are fit for book-agents—only a few being gifted with the necessary qualities.   Well, Fleming," he added, in his customary business-like manner, "you have begun so well that I suppose you will continue with us?"

I told him that I would; and being very greatly worn and fatigued, and anxious for a few hour's rest, I left my outfit to be called for next day and went out upon the street. A few blocks away, as I knew, there was an eating-house known as the Palace Restaurant, which was the most popular establishment of the kind in the city. Some three or four thousand people, it was said, got their meals there daily, and it was generally known that one could get a pretty fair meal there for fifteen or twenty cents. With my dollar in my pocket I went to this house and ordered a cheap but substantial meal, which I need not say was heartily enjoyed. This done, I repaired to a neighboring lodging-house, and though the sun would not set for another hour, I went to bed and slept until eight o'clock next day. I awoke greatly refreshed and after breakfast went to the Polyclinic Dispensary, a medical institution under the control of able and efficient physicians. I was treated here for diabetes mellitus, as long as I remained in San Francisco, and was finally pronounced cured by them.

From this place I returned to Mr. Underhill's office. Here I got my outfit and passed the day in canvassing about the city for orders. Good fortune seemed now to pursue me as persistently as dire misery had done. I took a sufficient number of orders to net me a handsome profit. I labored in this manner, day by day, for several months, and had many amusing experiences. My canvassing was done in a particular locality, and in making my selection, I followed instinct rather than reason. The most ultra-stylish and ultra-aristocratic quarter of the city was that known as Knob Hill. Nearly all of the class mentioned lived here, or in the immediate vicinity, and none others. They were an exclusive and purse-proud set, and Knob Hill had long been the terror of all book-salesmen I was told that no resident of Knob Hill, so far as was known, had ever purchased a book from an agent, and for years no salesman had been admitted into one of its exclusive mansions. Indeed, there was no agent bold enough to make the attempt. On all of the handsome residences which abounded in the vicinity, the eye was greeted by such notices, in glaring characters, as these:

"BOOK-CANVASSERS NOT ALLOWED." "BOOK-AGENTS AND TRAMPS, KEEP AWAY," and more to the same purpose. These signs were displayed in almost every conceivable place, and glared out upon the adventurous canvasser on every hand.

Now ever part of the city, with the single exception of Knob Hill, was completely overrun with enterprising book-agents, and competition was so brisk that none of them could earn more than a bare livelihood. And neither should I, had I followed in their course.

I turned my attention to Knob Hill; and from first to last, as long as I remained in San Francisco, I did almost all of my book-selling in that unpromising quarter. As might be expected, the other agents who saw fit to watch my course, prophesied my immediate and ignominious failure, but the croakings of such prophets of evil—of which the world is full—could not deter me from following my own plans. There were, as might be supposed, a few houses on the Hill more difficult to enter than some others; and one, in particular, had shown itself so hostile to all salesmen that the very sight of it was sufficient to make the boldest agent quake in his boots. I determined to enter this house first, and I did so.

It was a magnificent mansion, set in the midst of elegant and commodious grounds. Several signs, displayed on conspicuous parts of the basement, warned all book-agents in threatening language to keep away, and I own that it was not without misgivings that I entered and rang the bell. On entering the piazza, I placed my book and paper upon the floor and stood upon them. When the servant appeared, she seemed to suspect my errand, but I told her to tell her mistress that a newspaper man desired to see her. The servant turned about, without asking me to walk in, and closing the door, went away.

After a slight delay I heard, somewhat faintly, the majestic tread of a woman coming down the hall, and the rustle of silken garments. Then the door opened and the aristocratic and exclusive lady of the house stood before me. A tall woman, large, robust, and stout. Her complexion was coarse, her nose red, her features commonplace, while the expression upon her face was that of coarse, impertinent, and insolent vulgarity. I thought when this woman stood before me, and I noted the expression of her countenance, her air and manner, that she was one

of the most despicable of created beings, and an illus-
tration of upstart vulgarity in its most hateful and
repulsive form. My first impulse was to turn my back
upon her, and go on my way without more ado, but
such a course not appearing either very feasible or
very politic, I made her a low bow.

She came up to me without ceremony.

"So you're one of them reporter fellers?" Her
voice was loud, harsh, and unpleasant.

"I have the honor, madam," I responded, with
another bow, as graceful as I could make when standing upon a good-sized book, "to represent a newspaper."

She stared; then turning short about, with a
clownish attempt at graceful courtesy, but which was
only obsequious vulgarity, she told me to "come in."

She led the way; and, quickly snatching up my
book from the floor, and concealing it underneath
my coat, I followed her into a gorgeously-furnished
parlor. She waved her hand towards an elegantly
upholstered rocking-chair, and sank into a similar
seat herself. I then began to talk, and she listened
patiently enough until I drew out my book and paper.
As soon as her eyes fell upon these, she sprang up as
though the mere sight of a book had the same effect
upon her that a red flag has upon a bull, and approaching me threateningly, she exclaimed in a loud
angry voice:

"Are you one of them air book-agents?"

She pronounced the last word about as one would
speak the word rattlesnake.

"But, madam," said I, wishing to gain time, "if you will hear me—"

She interrupted me without ceremony.

"Are you one of them air book-agents? Air you?"

Then, without waiting for a reply she seized me by the collar, and by the exercise of simple muscular force, for she was almost twice as large as the unfortunate agent who was now in her clutches, she dragged me out into the hall, down the steps, and out into the yard until we stood before a glaring sign on which was painted the legend: "Book-agents not allowed on this place."

"Do you see that!" she shrieked, glaring down upon me more like a wild Indian about to take my scalp than a civilized American. "Do you see it, you dog?"

I was obliged to confess that I did.

"Well, then," said she, in a lower tone, releasing my collar from her grasp, "you remember it; and now you *git!* You rascal," she went on, as if her indignation at such a mortal affront mastered all other feelings whenever she thought of it, "you rascal, to deceive and insult a trustin' woman! You ought to be give sixty days. You villyun, to come sneakin' here! I thought you was a gentleman, and here you turn out a *book-agent.*" She spoke these words with ineffable scorn, and repeating it in the same tone several times over, she returned to the house, and disappeared behind the carved street door, her silken garments rustling angrily as she went.

There was nothing left for me but retreat, and

this more ignominiously than even my officious acquaintances had prophesied.   I need hardly say that I left with far less ceremony than I had observed when entering, but my poor success at this place did not deter me from trying similar places in that vicinity.   I canvassed all day on Knob Hill, taking my usual average of orders.   When I returned that afternoon to Mr. Underhill's office, he was very greatly surprised at my success, and complimented me very highly.

Shortly after my arrival in San Francisco I formed the habit of going regularly to the apartments of the Y. M. C. A.   Finally, some of the officers suggested that I deliver a public lecture in some of the churches of the city, and they offered to manage it for me. After deliberating over the matter for some time, I decided to make the attempt, and a month or so after I had returned an affirmative answer, the lecture was announced. We had a good audience, and the church was filled. As to what others thought of the lecture, and the general effect it had, perhaps I cannot do better than simply to reproduce here, begging pardon of the reader, the following head lines which appeared next day in a leading morning newspaper over the reporter's account of the affair.

A SENSATIONAL LECTURE.

MISSION STREET CHURCH CROWDED TO OVERFLOWING.

E. B. FLEMING, OF TEXAS, DELIVERED THE FOLLOW-

ING REMARKABLE, UNIQUE AND POWERFUL

ADDRESS TO A LARGE AUDIENCE

LAST NIGHT.

While this was very encouraging, the amount of the money-receipts was no less gratifying, of which my share amounted to about thirty dollars.   I lectured after this in various parts of the State, and always with the most unexpected though gratifying success.

I then left the city of San Francisco and journeyed per steamer down the coast, stopping, among other places, at Santa Barbara, San Luis Obispo, and ultimately at San Diego.   At the latter place I remained nearly a year.

CHAPTER XII.

'Tis sweet to hear the watchdog's honest bark
　　Bay deop-mouthed welcome as we draw near home
'Tis sweet to know there is an eye will mark
　　Our coming, and look brighter when we come.
　　　　　　　　　　　　　　　—*Byron.*

The city of San Diego is one of the prettiest places
in the west. It stands on the coast, near the monu-
ment that divides the two Republics. I lodged at
the Holt House and went about the city canvassing
for the publications of P. F. Collier. On one occasion I inadvertently entered the house of a minister
of the gospel named Jones. I was selling, among
other things, the novels of Bulwer-Lytton, Cooper,
Dickens and Scott. The Rev. Mr. Jones became
very much incensed when I offered to sell him sets of
these works, and accused me of demoralizing the city
by putting such books in the homes of the people.

I saw him on the streets quite often after that and
he never failed to hit a verbal blow at my business,
or to sneer at me, or to remind me of my "wickedness"
as he called it, for selling novels. He was a pompous
man, and paraded the streets with the grandest air
imaginable, and this, together with his bigoted per-

229

tinacity in pursuing me, were the occasion of my deciding upon a way to humble him a little. One night I wrote a sentence, something after the style of those in the Bible, and determined to give him. a public opportunity to explain it to me. The sentence ran thus: "And Paul said, Get ye down, and whether ye revenge let it be mystified into eternal as well as increatable contrition."

One day I was standing upon the sidewalk among a crowd of acquaintances when the Rev. Mr. Jones came stepping grandly by.

"Parson," said I, detaining him in such a position that the crowd could hear, and speaking in a distinct voice, "I have a sentence here which I should be glad to have you explain, and tell me what book or epistle in the Bible it is from."

"Why certainly," he replied, loftily, "I shall be quite glad to do so."

I thereupon handed him the slip whereon I had written the sentence. He took it, read the words over to himself in a low voice, and then repeated them for the benefit of those looking on.

"That," said the preacher, in a pompous tone, "is from Paul. I have seen it quite often. It simply repeats a lesson the inspired Book often enjoins, to be humble and reverent in the sight of God, and is in perfect keeping with the rest of the Scriptures."

He then launched out into a long, impromptu sermon upon these points, referring to the sentence frequently, and explaining its different points. When he had done this, he seemed to feel that he had

accomplished a very wonderful feat indeed, and became more pompous than ever. He handed the slip
back to me and was about to pass on.

"Parson," said I, "do you remember the exact
chapter in the Bible in which this sentence occurs?"

"Well, no," he admitted, knitting his brows, "I
think, however, that it will be found in the first
epistle of Paul."

"I cannot agree with you," said I. "Furthermore,
I will give any man ten dollars who will find this
sentence *anywhere* in the Bible."

"What do you mean?" says Mr. Preacher, growing
very red.

"I simply mean that this sentence is not in the
Bible, and never was."

"Do you intend, sir," cried he, "to utter blasphe-
mies against God's Holy Word?"

"By no means," I responded. "I have no such
intention. On the contrary, I simply mean to take
part of the conceit out of a man who does not practice the religion he preaches. Sir, I wrote this
sentence myself, last night."

A great laugh went up at this; and the preacher,
darting at me a glance which expressed anything but
love, or good will, turned about and hurried off down
the street.

During my stay in San Diego I received the local
newspapers from my old Texas home, and as they
invariably reached me on a certain day, I always
looked forward to that hour with anxious pleasure.
One day as I came out of the postoffice with one of

these papers a young man was standing dejectedly on the sidewalk. I had seen him quite often, and we were something more than mere acquaintances He bade me good morning, and looked so pale and wan and melancholy, that I asked him if he was ill.

He replied, "No," and smiled in a sickly manner.

I went on down the street towards the city park, which was only a block or so away, to have a quiet hour with the news from home so eagerly longed for. The young man followed me, and we sat down upon the same seat. But in my selfish joy at hearing from home I almost turned my back upon him, and began to read my paper. While I was intent upon this employment, and without the least warning, a pistol shot rang out so near to me that I did not know for a moment whether I was shot or not, and a cloud of smoke from the burning powder swept across my face. At the same time, I heard a groan. I sprang up in alarm.

Then I saw that my late companion was not upon the seat, but had fallen to the ground. A smoking pistol was clutched convulsively in his hand, and I saw at once that the unfortunate young man had taken his own life. A ghastly bullet-hole gaped in his head, and blood was trickling from it. As I bent over him, I heard excited cries and the tramp of many feet. He was quite dead, the bullet having penetrated his brain.

At this moment I was seized, and a voice cried into my ear: "What did you shoot this man for?"

I lookd up, and saw myself surrounded by an excited crowd. A policeman had seized my arm, but did not prevent me from rising to my feet.

"I did not kill him," I said to the officer, "can't you see that he killed himself?"

"A thin tale," some one sneered. "Officer, I advise you to hold that man."

"And I advise *jou*, my friend," said I, "not to meddle with things you know nothing of."

By this time a man, evidently one in authority, had come up. He glanced around him keenly.

"What are you holding this man for?" he said to the policeman. "Release him. Can't you see that it is a clear case of suicide? Friend," he said to me, "you may go. But hold. Give me your name. We may need you."

I gave him my name, and, being free to go, did not remain a single moment.

During my sojourn in San Diego I came very unexpectedly upon two old Texas friends, Mr. James N. Cook, and Sim T. Hartsfield, and received many kind favors from them. They yet reside in California.

As has been stated, I remained in San Diego for nearly a year, and my health steadily improved. Before this time had elapsed, however, I had begun to think of returning to my Texas home, feeling able to cope with the trying climate of that section. It was in March of the year 1890 that I returned to Texas and was reunited with my family.

The storms and tumult of an eventful life have passed away, and the calm that precedes the end of all has come.   In the evening of my days I can look back over the unquiet ocean, and the rugged steeps that lie behind, and lo! the hours of darkness and storm have gone forever.   I have passed them, and the lengthening shadows that, stealing closer, announce the coming of perpetual night, are begnining to gather about me.   Yet despite the deepening shadows, I can yet see, in the blue void above me, whence the long reaches of ominous clouds have rolled away, the wide sky shining calmly and serenely down upon me.

THE END

www.ingramcontent.com/pod-product-compliance
Lightning Source LLC
Chambersburg PA
CBHW020109030726
47498CB00006B/2028